LONDON
STORIES

LONDON STORIES

Three Emily Castles Mysteries

HELEN SMITH

Sign up for Helen Smith's Book News and get a FREE Kindle copy of one of Helen Smith's books. Go here to learn more: http://eepurl.com/ssbf5

These stories were first published separately:
Three Sisters|Showstoppers|Real Elves
Now collected into one bundle of fun!

For Erna May and Eric

INDEX

THREE SISTERS

The south London sky exploded with a thousand deaths that night. Emily looked up. Tiny coloured lights hung in the blackness, like Midget Gems suspended mid-rinse in a toddler's open mouth. She was on her way to the bonfire party at the big house at the end of the street in Brixton, where she lived, at the invitation of the new owner, whom she had never met. Emily should have been used to the fireworks at her age because there had always been fireworks on bonfire night, for as long as she could remember — the fireworks now as much a celebration of Diwali, the Hindu festival of light; and Halloween, the American festival of gore and dressing up; as Guy Fawkes Night, when people in England remembered the day back in 1605 when a plot had been foiled that, had it been successful, would have blown up the Houses of Parliament, with King James I inside it.

But tonight each explosion startled Emily slightly, as if it was the sound of a gunshot, danger. And the sizzling sausage smell of blackening flesh that hung in the autumn air made her think of her dog, Jessie, who had died the week before. The dog had not been barbecued: she died peacefully, after a long and happy life. But she had very much enjoyed eating sausages.

Emily was carrying a tray of homemade cheesy potato bake – a wholesome, portable dish that usually went down well at parties – and a bottle of rosé wine. Ordinarily she wouldn't have gone. Ordinarily, she would have been at home with Jessie, just in case the dog was disturbed by the noise of the fireworks. But those days were gone. And when the handwritten invitation had been slipped through her letterbox, well, she had interpreted it as a sign that she should start a new life and find some new friends. How was she to know she was making an appointment, not just with a new life, but with death?

Halloween had fallen this year on the weekend before bonfire night, and as usual, many people were out celebrating both events. Local children wandered the streets in ugly masks. At least, she hoped they were masks. For a moment or two Emily felt uneasy – what if this invitation was some sort of trick? What if she got to the big house at the end of the street and the place was dark and deserted? But then she seemed to feel the presence of her dog, Jessie, walking beside her for a few paces, and she felt reassured.

As she got closer to the house, she saw it was not deserted. First she heard music, and then she saw the coloured lights strung up in the trees, and finally she heard the happy buzz of conversation from people gathered in the garden. The guests were easily distinguishable from their hosts because they wore anoraks, scarves and gloves. The hosts were walking on stilts or juggling fire – the first sight Emily had was of a giant, glowing, pink papier-mâché or fibreglass painted head floating about five feet above the top of the privet hedge that surrounded the property.

Like most people who live in London, Emily didn't know her neighbours very well, though she knew most by sight and some by name – usually because she'd had to take in parcels or bouquets of flowers when they were out. She recognised Dr. Muriel walking through the gates just ahead of her, pulling a small two-wheeled shopping trolley with one hand and tapping at the pavement for support every three or four paces or so with an elegant silver-topped cane in the other. Dr. Muriel was a hearty, squarish woman the colour of concrete. She lived in one of the red brick Edwardian houses opposite Emily's flat. Emily had taken in mail order deliveries of large parcels of nutritious bird seed from the RSPB for Dr. Muriel. Now, as she followed her, she imagined Dr. Muriel standing very still in her garden with her cupped hands outstretched, wild birds perched along her sleeves as if she were a washing line, waiting their turn to peck at the sunflower seeds and other delicious avian titbits while their benefactor cheeped and chirruped to them in a language they seemed to understand. Though it would have been a sight to behold, Emily had never seen anything like this happen, she only imagined it.

To her left, as Emily walked into the garden where the bonfire party was being held, she saw a monkey puzzle tree strung with coloured light bulbs, as dangerous – with its sharp prickles and damp electric wires – as a cheaply-made, faulty, imported, artificial Christmas tree. Next to the tree stood a tall, thin woman with curly hair, who was another neighbour of Emily. Emily knew her name was Victoria and she had three male children who were fond of skateboarding. Victoria was preoccupied with chasing a cube of potato salad across a cream-coloured cardboard plate with a fragile-looking white plastic fork. She didn't look up when Emily passed. One of her duffle-coated children stared out at Emily through a wolf mask while bending his knees and sliding his back up and down against his mother's trouser leg, like a donkey relieving an itch on a fence post. Without taking her eye off her meal, his mother bent and murmured something to him, and he stood still and looked up at her and away from Emily.

It was a very cold, dark night, and the air was damp, but there was no rain. The conditions were perfect for the party, and the garden was filled with people determined to enjoy themselves, clumped near the fire bowls and coloured lanterns for warmth and light, and ooh-ing and aah-ing at the stilt-walkers and jugglers. They swapped spurious, conflicting pieces of information: the stilt-walkers were Polish, the jugglers were Scottish, the artist who had made the giant head was Spanish, it was a squat party, it was illegal, it was sanctioned by the local council, it was bankrolled by Sir Paul

McCartney. Most of it was nonsense, but some of it was true.

A man and a woman Emily didn't know stood at the bottom of the three or four stone steps that led up to the door to the house, sipping at cinnamon-scented mulled wine from white plastic cups and smoking cigarettes. They smiled at Emily as she passed, and she saw that the woman's lips were painted red, and her teeth had been stained the colour of blackberries by the wine. Her brown fuzzy hair had been teased into an unflattering triangular shape, and she seemed to have pencilled her eyebrows in without looking in a mirror.

'If you want the baby,' said the man to the woman, 'have the baby. Or sell it. I don't care.'

The woman shrieked. She seemed deranged. The man dropped his cigarette and grabbed at her. Emily stopped on the top step and turned, ready to intervene. But the woman let him put his arms around her. She smooched with him, rubbing the fox fur collar of her long black coat against his shoulder, and the two of them turned slowly in each other's arms, like lovers dancing on a music box, as she began to sing the chorus of 'La Vie en Rose'. People standing nearby recognised the tune and came a little closer to listen. Some of them clapped. Emily moved on.

Inside the house was a grand hall so large that it was served by two staircases. The plaster on the walls was cracked, and there was a slight smell of mildew, but the flagstones on the floor had been scrubbed, and the place had been fixed up with chandeliers hanging from the ceiling and original artwork on the walls. A man in a cape and a top hat swooshed past – he was young, no more than twenty-one or twenty-two, and he was wearing a false moustache, and he had rouged his cheeks. He tipped his hat at Emily. 'Madame,' he said. Emily smiled weakly. A heavy wooden door opened on the opposite side of the hall, and as two laughing teenage girls emerged, Emily saw that they had come from the kitchen, and she headed there to leave her offerings.

The kitchen was bare, pretty much, except for a large porcelain sink and a cream-coloured fridge that was taller than Emily and twice as wide. And there were two trestle tables, one stacked with bottles of booze, a large pot of mulled wine that was being heated over a small portable gas burner, and a bowl of punch. The other was laden with dishes prepared by the hosts or brought by the guests: macaroni cheese, mince pies, quiches, pasta salads, rice salads, tuna salads, potato salads, baked potatoes, garlic bread – and an assortment of minced pork, beef and lamb products in the form of sausages, scotch eggs, a cottage pie, and chilli con carne. Everything was on the spectrum from brown to cream, and the overall effect was of a sepia-toned display that had been put together by someone nostalgic for a time before Britons had learned to cook, but after they had learned to shop at supermarkets.

'What a spread!' said Dr. Muriel, with the jovial sincerity of a popular visitor to an old people's home or a primary school. 'Wouldn't it be fun to try and guess who has brought what?'

Emily edged her cheesy potato bake onto the table next to the scotch eggs, thinking it wouldn't be fun at all; her dish had already congealed slightly, and the top was glazing over, as if she had persisted in telling it a very dull story on the way here. From her trolley, Dr. Muriel brought a bottle of port, two dozen homemade mince pies and a large round Stilton cheese. 'Low self-esteem is often caused by low blood sugar,' she said, filling a plate with a selection from the buffet. 'It's a good idea to eat well at parties.'

A young woman in a belted mac approached Emily. She was very, very thin with dark, short hair held back with a clip with tiny glass beads on it that nobody could possibly have mistaken for real jewels, and she came so close that Emily could smell the wardrobe smell on her coat. The flesh under her cheekbones was scooped out, like a jack-o'-lantern, but prettier.

'My name is Elise. Can you help me? I need to get a message to our friend, but I'm being watched. I have information that is vital, *vital*, to the success of our joint endeavour.'

Emily looked around uncertainly, and then she looked back at Elise, who was staring at her intently.

'What's the message, m'dear?' asked Dr. Muriel.

'The message is in the suitcase.'

'And who's it for? Who's our friend?'

Elise looked surprised at the question. 'Why, the gentleman who is waiting for the suitcase, of course.' She turned to leave. Then she stopped and held up one finger. She looked at Emily. 'Could you

9

help me get the suitcase to the gentleman?' she asked.

Emily said, 'Well, I...' She shrugged. Then Elise shrugged – she might have been mimicking or mocking Emily. 'Maybe later,' Emily said.

Elise gave her a look of such desperate longing that Emily felt embarrassed. Elise turned and walked away, moving slowly, with dignity, like someone who is used to being watched.

Dr. Muriel looked for somewhere to put her plate down so that she could applaud as Elise walked away. There was no space on the trestle table so she held on to the plate and thumped the top of her left hand with her right, as if she were trying to knock clods of mud from her wellington boots. Marvellous!' she said. 'Marvellous!'

At the door that led to the grand hall, Elise turned and inclined her head. Then she was gone. Even though it had only been make-believe, Emily still felt involved, guilty.

More guests came into the kitchen. Some were wearing fancy dress – but even when their costumes were hired, the guests were easily distinguishable from their hosts. Their hosts moved purposefully through the rooms like characters pouring into the party from an alternate world, obeying rules and impulses and reacting to events and objects that only they could interpret, whereas their guests were just ordinary people who were standing about, enjoying the various 'entertainments', but contributing nothing.

It was somehow a metaphor for life, but Emily couldn't see what she was supposed to learn from it. She was too old to run away and join a theatre troupe. Anyway, for now, something else was bothering her. 'I never know what to say or even if we're supposed to join in.'

'Nerve-wracking, isn't it!' said Dr. Muriel. She didn't look nervous at all; she looked as if she could stand and face a charging rhino.

Emily left her and went to explore.

The dilapidated house had been done up quickly and efficiently at very low cost, furnished with furniture from skips and material salvaged from jumble sales, and decorated with original artworks created by members of the collective who had occupied the place. Emily's favourite so far was an oxidised metal sculpture of the skeleton of a horse. It seemed to be galloping along one of the balconies, where Emily had looked up and seen it from the ground floor.

Nails and staples were visible in the furnishings if you looked close up, but from a distance the effects were grand, theatrical, striking. Emily was impressed with the transformation – she had often walked past on her way to work, head down, not looking forward to her day, or head down, hurrying to get home again to Jessie. If she had thought about the house at all, she had only thought that it was a shame that the place was slowly rotting away. Now she could see that something wonderful had been achieved with determination and an entrepreneurial spirit. Was it because they were risk-takers? Was it because they had gathered here from all over the world, a group of culturally diverse people pooling their resources harmoniously to achieve success? Emily climbed the stairs to have a look around on the first floor. From what she had observed at the party so far, most of her hosts were engaged in dangerous activities – walking on stilts, juggling with fire – of the kind that she had been warned against as a child. Had they never been warned? Was she seeing the product of neglectful childhoods? Or was she witnessing a collective rebellion? Whichever it was, she was astounded by the results.

Even as Emily was pondering this, a young woman came running up behind her in a corridor with *not just one* but a dozen knives in her hand. Emily stood very still, a deer in a forest. But the woman ran past. She was a slim woman – young enough to be called a girl, still – with dyed blonde hair. She was wearing a blue-grey spangled circus-style costume that was rather tatty close up – stained under the armpits, slightly frayed at the groin, and with loose threads where sequins were missing.

The knives she was carrying had short, stubby blades and ornate handles – probably they'd be better described as daggers, rather than knives. The girl ran full-tilt into one of the rooms further along the corridor. Emily followed, curious. Perhaps there was to be another entertainment. Emily opened the door and peeped in. The room had been done out like a frou-frou boudoir, with swathes of pink velvet draped above a very large bed, gilt mirrors on the walls, and a fancy white and gilt dressing table with a very large hole smashed in the side, as if someone had kicked it. That was the only clue that it might have been rescued from a skip (though, of course, it could have been damaged recently in an argument). The gilt mirrors were spotted and cloudy, and their frames were chipped. But at a glance, the decorative effect was decadent and appealing. The girl with the knives lay on the bed – the knives were in a box next to her. She looked thunderously angry, registering emotions of the sort of intensity that might easily have resulted in a piece of furniture being kicked. Another blonde girl in a slightly less tatty blue-grey costume sat on a pink velvet-upholstered chair in front of the dressing table. She touched up her make-up, leaning in toward the gilt mirror propped above it, flicking at her lashes with mascara, her lipsticked mouth a pornographic O. Emily noticed that there were surprisingly few things on the dressing table – just a hairbrush, a jar of foundation, a big pink pot of blusher with a long-handled brush to apply it, and an uncapped red lipstick in a gorgeously old-fashioned gold casing.

At first sight, because of their matching costumes, hair colour and make-up, the two girls looked almost identical, but as Emily looked from one to the other, she began to see differences – this one had higher cheekbones, that one had fuller lips, and so on. It was disconcerting because the dressing room mirror was angled so that Emily could see into it from the doorway. The result was that Emily could see three near-identical faces, though there were only two sisters in the room.

As Emily was gawping at the sisters, the door to the en suite bathroom opened to the boastful sound of the toilet flushing, and Emily's Japanese neighbour Midori stepped into the bedroom. The flushing continued loudly. It sounded like applause. Midori certainly deserved it: She was wearing white PVC hotpants, long white clumpy boots, white eyeshadow, pale pink lipstick. She came towards Emily with a smile, shaking her still-damp hands as if she hadn't been able to find the guest towel. Even if she'd improvised by wiping her hands on her clothes, as Emily might have done, there would have been no point: she was wearing nothing absorbent.

The sisters looked up at Midori, apparently unaware that she'd been using the facilities, and then they looked at Emily. They didn't seem pleased to see either of them.

'Zizi!' said the girl with the knives to her sister.

Zizi got up from the dressing table. As Midori stepped out of the bedroom past where Emily stood gawking in the doorway, Zizi shut the door in Emily's face. It seemed unnecessarily rude – but then again, it could have been part of a performance.

'Heh!' Emily said to Midori, by way of acknowledging that this place was exciting, but also really rather unsettling.

Midori said, 'Emily, right?'

'Yeah. We live on the same street.'

'I seen you with your dog. Very old.'

'She died.'

'Oh. I'm sorry, Emily.'

'That's OK. You look nice, Midori. I wish I'd dressed up a bit.'

'I'm DJ. I'm playing tonight – only neighbour involved in the party. Very exciting.' She twisted her hands and linked her fingers together, and then she moved her hands up and down a few times, as if attempting a handshake of self-congratulation.

'Hey,' said Emily. 'That's great, Midori!'

'I got a DJ stage name: "Hana-bi" – Japanese name. You know what it means?' Emily obviously didn't look like much of a linguist because Midori didn't wait for her to reply before supplying the answer. '"Fireworks". The words say "fire flowers."'

'That's lovely.'

'I'm on in a half hour – going to the kitchen to have a bite to eat. You wanna come?'

'Yeah, why not? Food's always comforting at a party.'

'Those sisters upset you, Emily? Very rude.'

'No. It's fine.'

So Emily went down to the kitchen with Midori to have a bit of food. The kitchen was crowded this time, with people lining up to put food on their plates. Emily cheered up a bit, and then she saw that her cheesy potato bake hadn't gone down well. It was rather grey and congealed, and she overheard one of the other revellers being rather rude about it. She recognised him as one of the Australian lads who lived on her street.

'What do you make of that, Jake?' he said to his friend.

'It's proof of life on the moon,' said Jake. 'It *is* made of cheese – and grey rocks. And some scientist is gonna be sorry his wife has raided his lab and brought a sample of his work to the party instead of the shepherd's pie she was supposed to bring.'

'Oh, hey, shepherd's pie? I wouldn't mind some of that. Can you see any? Wahey, Chris! Great party.'

This last remark was addressed to a fair-haired English man who was eating a green apple. He nodded.

'Midori,' said Chris. 'You're all set up outside, whenever you're ready. You OK for food?' The pyramid of food teetering on Midori's plate suggested that this was so. 'You want a drink? You want a glass of punch?' He ladled some punch into a paper cup and handed it over. 'How about your friend?'

'Emily,' said Emily. 'No, I don't think so. Thank you.'

'Chris is in charge,' said Midori. 'Party's his idea.'

'So you sent the invitation?' said Emily.

Chris said, 'Not personally.'

'I didn't expect you to be English. I thought everyone in this... collective... was Spanish or Polish or...'

'Yeah. All except me.'

'So you all chipped in to buy this place?'

'We don't go in for ownership. We've got a network around the world to help us identify abandoned spaces. We identify, occupy, beautify – we fix it up and make one little corner of the world a prettier place. And then we move on. We've been on the road for a long time.'

'And now you've come home,' said Emily.

'Home?' said Chris. 'Home is where the art is, Emily.'

He had an intense way of looking at her, as though he was assessing her worth – and had found her wanting. She didn't like his slightly sardonic way of talking. She found she disliked him. But what was it she objected to? His intensity or his flippancy? Or just the way he looked at her. She hated to admit that there was nothing intellectual about her reaction – she was probably just out of sorts after overhearing Jake's comments about the food she had made.

Emily wanted to get away from the kitchen, but Chris was still here, hemming her in by the buffet. 'Are you enjoying the party?' he asked.

'I am. I never know what's going to happen next.'

'It's all great. Just don't miss the knife throwing.'

'Is that the sisters? Zizi and...?'

'Zizi and Zsa-Zsa. They're awesome.'

'Yeah. They didn't think much of Midori using their bathroom while they were trying to get ready.'

'Did she? Where was that? Upstairs?'

'I tried to get a look in case it was a performance, like Elise–'

'Ah, poor Elise. I wonder if she's got anyone to take her suitcase to that man yet.'

'She asked me. Was I supposed to say yes?'

'Yes.'

'So which one is it who throws the knives? Is it Zizi or Zsa-Zsa?'

'You'll have to see it to find out,' Chris said. He looked amused.

'There's no audience participation, is there? They both looked in such a mardy mood just now, I don't think I'd want to take my chances.'

Chris smirked. The expression made his nose look very long and straight, and his mouth looked strangely sexy. Emily thought she had detected in Chris's accent and demeanour a sense of entitlement that only comes from rich, well-educated people – the sort who can afford to go swanning off around the world with a troupe of performers in the name of art. *If you were really so well brought-up,* Emily thought, *you might ask 'do you mind if I smirk?' before puffing your condescension all over me.* But then she remembered her dog had just died, and probably that was making her thin-skinned and emotional, and she was at a party, and she seemed to have forgotten how to enjoy herself, and she had better start.

And then a tall, dark-haired man edged in next to her at the buffet table and took charge of things, as though he had heard her silent command to get the party started. 'Joe,' said Chris, nodding in acknowledgement. Was there a hint of antagonism in the way he said Joe's name?

'OK, man,' Joe said. He was strong-looking, as though he worked outdoors, and he spoke with a slight accent. He turned away from Chris, and as he turned away – he was half a head taller than Emily, so she had to tilt up to get a good look at his handsome face – she saw something she hadn't been expecting to see in response to Chris's antagonism. Not bitterness or aggression or anger or indifference. No, for a moment she thought Joe looked sad.

'You got to eat something,' Joe said, noticing Emily's empty plate. He put a huge spoonful of her cheesy potato bake on her plate, and then he put an equally good portion of it on his. 'It's good,' he said, as if she needed persuading. 'We make it like this at home in Hungary. You have the meat, and you have

21

the potatoes. I don't understand this *layers* of things,' he indicated the dish of lasagne and the dish of cottage pie, 'like they want to hide the meat in there because it's shy.'

He looked towards Midori, but her plate was full. She stood and scoffed her food right there in the kitchen in a ladylike but extremely efficient manner, plate to her chin, fork to mouth, fork to mouth, fork to mouth. With her crazy white gear and her repetitive movements, she could have been a next-generation robot demonstrating hoovering techniques.

'Ah. Better,' she said when she was almost done. She put her plate down and used both hands to snap the heads off two prawns that remained on it, then sucked the meat out of the prehistoric little bodies like a very genteel predator.

'You want some punch?' Joe said to Midori. He put a paper cup down on the table next to her.

'Got some.' She took an individually-wrapped, alcohol-soaked hand wipe from the pink plastic bag that was slung over her shoulder, the cartoon cats depicted on it bouncing at her hip, and she ripped open the packaging and carefully wiped all eight fingers and two thumbs on her hands like a proud mama. She swigged the cup of punch down in two draughts, and then she went out into the garden where her DJ booth had been set up.

Joe loaded up his plate with meatballs and salad, and every time he took something for himself, he first offered a serving of it to Emily. He took two paper napkins and two plastic forks from the table. He said, 'You want to go outside and eat?'

Emily did. She had formed rather a good first impression of Joe, with his strong, muscular arms and his air of slight sadness. Added to that, he had been nice about the food she had brought.

Emily and Joe went and sat together on two plastic chairs in the enormous garden. It was much bigger than any of the other gardens Emily had glimpsed from her street. It was much bigger than her garden, which she tended lovingly in spite of the difficulties of maintaining a lush green lawn that arose from allowing an elderly Golden Retriever to piddle on the grass a couple of times a day.

The party house had once been a very grand house, and the size of the garden where Emily and Joe were now sitting was testament to that. There was a small orchard off to the west of the garden, with apple, cherry and pear trees in it. Nearer the house were neglected flower beds with overgrown shrubs and bushes, and midway between house and orchard, on what had once probably been a very fine lawn, there was a towering bonfire that had not yet been lit. It was stacked with sawn-up pieces of wood, branches and kindling. Emily surmised that it had been built by a man because in her experience men were good at making fires (goodness knows, she was self-sufficient, but building a decent fire in the grate in the decorative but functional tiled fireplace in her flat was the one thing she never quite managed to do to her own satisfaction).

Close to the house was Midori in her DJ booth, a temporary structure decorated with fairy lights and bearing a hand-painted sign with 'DJ Hana-bi' on it. Closer still was a barbecue with a man in a chef's hat, an apron and checked trousers. He was carving roast pork from a pig on a spit and serving it to a very long line of hungry customers. Emily wondered if there was any difference, ethically, between eating a dog and eating a pig. If so, then whether or not it was acceptable to eat a two-year-old child was another question that ought to be considered as part of the mix: Emily had read that dogs were supposed to be just as intelligent as toddlers, and she had read that pigs were cleverer still.

Emily didn't think she ought to share with Joe her thoughts about pigs, dogs and toddlers. She didn't want to allude to her assumption that he must be good at lighting fires as he was a man. She didn't want to sit there and imagine him chopping up pieces of wood with an axe in his hands. She didn't want to sound as though she was being suggestive or simpering at him.

'Did you build that bonfire?' she asked Joe.

'I helped,' he said.

She pressed on, trying to find a bonfire-related question that didn't involve a mention of chopping, smoking, lighting fires... she came up with, 'I hope you checked for hedgehogs this morning, if it's been there overnight. You know, they crawl in there and sleep if it looks cosy?'

'Hedgehogs, horses, people. We checked it, don't worry. When they light it, there's gonna be a big parade. They're gonna put an effigy on the fire and burn it. You're gonna stay and see it?'

'Oh, yes. And the knife throwing. I want to see that, too.'

'Yeah? Why?'

'I heard it was good. Zizi and...'

'Zizi and Zsa-Zsa. Crazy girls. Yeah, it's one hell of an act.'

'What do you do here... Joe?'

'Joszef. You can call me Joe.'

'Do you have an act, Joe?'

'No, Emily. It's Emily, right?'

She was eating a meatball, but she bobbed her chin up and down, acknowledging that he was right.

He said, 'I don't put on a mask. I make some of the props. The art works – did you see the metal horse upstairs? I made that. I used to be a blacksmith in my hometown. So now I do this.'

'Where's home?'

'Hungary. What about you, Emily? You from here?'

'Yeah, I'm... I'm one of the neighbours. One of the guests. I live on this street. I'm not from London, though. But this is a city of immigrants, isn't it? Nearly everyone's moved here from somewhere, including me. Though I only moved from the countryside – no need for a passport.'

'You OK, Emily?'

'Do I look miserable? My dog just died.'

'Oh, that's a shame.'

'Well, everyone who has a dog; it dies eventually. I just need to get over it.'

'That's OK – it just happened... didn't it?'

'Yes. And I've been moping about the house the last few days, and I realised I'd been operating for years as one half of a human/dog duo. I need to get used to life without the furrier half. The separation is so real, I can feel it. If you had a diagram of the human body here now, I could point to the place where the wound would run from just beneath my armpit to just above my thigh – as if there was some kind of physical manifestation of the separation from Jessie.'

'I don't have a diagram of the human body, Emily.'

'I don't have any outward scar.'

'Oh, OK. I wondered if you were going to ask me whether I wanted to see it.'

Emily thought, *Are you flirting with me, Joe?* She blushed. She looked at his neck where his shirt was open – the only naked part of him that she could see. He had a gold chain around his neck and some dark hairs on the region below the collarbone where his neck officially became his chest. She wondered if he had any scars that he would like her to see.

27

Joe said, 'I got to get some props ready for the girls.'

'The knife-throwing girls?'

'Uh huh.' He grinned. He gripped her bicep as if they were two men who'd just shared a pint, and he said, 'You take care of yourself, Emily.'

He walked off towards the house, leaving behind his plate and plastic cutlery. *You're not perfect, then,* thought Emily. She picked up his plate and hers, so she could tidy up, and she looked at the grease on her hands and under her fingernails. She would have been grateful for one of those individually-wrapped alcohol-soaked hand towels just then, and thinking of it made her look towards Midori, which is how she happened to be watching her friend just when it happened: There were three or four explosions from a neighbouring garden as firework rockets went off, and Emily jumped and thought about gunshots – and then Midori went down. The Japanese girl dropped, as if someone had taken hold of the edges of her and was trying to shake her down like a duvet and hadn't held on tightly enough to the corners. It didn't look as though it was something she was in control of personally. It didn't look as though she was ducking or dancing or reaching for a record from the case at her feet. It looked as though she had been shot.

Oh my God! thought Emily. *She's down!* And her next thought was that she sounded ridiculous. And then she started running towards the DJ booth, hoping that Midori was only looking for something and would pop up again in a minute and carry on. The music continued, of course, because Midori's job involved changing the records, not cranking a machine to keep them spinning round. Emily got to the booth, and Midori was on the floor, apparently unconscious. There was no blood, and she was breathing. The two Aussies, Jake and the other one, whatever his name was – the rude one – had seen what had happened and reached Midori at about the same time.

'What happened?' Jake asked Emily.

Emily said, 'I don't know. I was watching, and she just went down. She hasn't been shot?'

'What d'you reckon, Rob?' Jake said to his friend, and Rob said, 'She's fainted, mate. Maybe it was something she ate – a dodgy prawn?'

Rob took hold of Midori under the armpits and hauled her out of the DJ booth, then he shifted her up into his arms, so her chest was on his chest, and carried her with her head on his shoulder towards the house. And meanwhile Jake stepped into Midori's place, selected the next record to be played, and lined it up and mixed it in seamlessly. The music continued, and nobody who hadn't witnessed it would have known that anything had happened at all. From the nonchalant way Jake and Rob behaved, it seemed this must be a fairly regular occurrence in the outback or wherever they had grown up, something they had been drilled in, the way children on fault lines are told what to do if there is an earthquake, except that their particular fault line required that they should step in at a moment's notice to DJ at artistic parties, or carry around unconscious Japanese women in white PVC hotpants.

Emily followed Rob as he carried Midori towards a side entrance to the house, just along from the kitchen. Presumably this entrance had once been a servants' entrance. It was poorly lit and out of sight from the party, bordered by a herb garden, and what had presumably once been a vegetable patch, though it was now overgrown with weeds.

As they stepped through the mud in the dark, Emily looked over at the brightly lit front door that led directly to the grand hall. Rob must have caught her look. 'Don't want to make a fuss, eh?' he said to Emily, by way of explanation. And it was true that if he had carried Midori through the grand hall in front of all their neighbours, there would have been an awful fuss. But he tried the side door, and it wouldn't open, so then Emily tried it too. As Emily was rattling the handle, without any luck, Midori stirred a little on Rob's chest and vomited. But because Rob was pretty quick about setting her down and lying her in the recovery position and because the vomit had come out in an arc, none of it went on any of them, it just puddled into the grass.

'She's pretty crook, eh?' said Rob.

'Should I get a doctor?' said Emily.

'What about Dr. Muriel?'

Dr. Muriel was a capable woman, but she was a doctor of ethics and had no medical training, so far as Emily knew. She might have been the person to ask about whether it was any better to eat a pig than a dog or a toddler, but even if she'd been available to answer the question, this probably wasn't quite the right time to ask.

'Midori?' said Emily. And then again, 'Midori!' She said to Rob, 'I wonder if I should take her to hospital.'

Just then Midori opened her eyes and wiped her mouth with the back of her hand and said, 'Aw. Sorry about that, Rob.'

'Can you stand up?' Rob asked her.

Midori stood, a little shakily.

Rob said, 'This was gonna be your big night.'

'I know.'

'Come on, I'll get you a glass of water, and then I'll walk you home.'

'Do you want me to come?' said Emily.

'No, you're all right,' said Rob.

'It's OK, Emily,' Midori said. 'You stay at the party. I'm gonna go lie down.'

'What could have made you so ill?'

'Punch,' said Midori.

'You only had two swigs of it.'

'Well I'm glad I stayed away from it,' said Rob, 'because it must be lethal. Mate, it's really done you in.'

He took his scarf off and put it around Midori's neck. He took his jacket off and put Midori's arms into the sleeves as though she was a child who needed help getting ready for school – right arm first, that's it. Then the left. Midori was shivering. Rob put his arm around her shoulder and steered her towards home.

Emily wandered a little further up around the side of the house, away from the front door. It was quiet here – or at least, though she could hear the music, there was no one else around – and she was trying to decide whether or not she should go home or stay at the party. She felt she ought to stay and try to enjoy herself now that she didn't have to go home for Jessie. Dear old Jessie – what would she want Emily to do? Emily heard, then, the sound of a dog whimpering. Now, Emily was an imaginative person, but she wasn't suggestible, and she didn't believe in ghosts. She knew it wasn't Jessie trying to communicate with her from the afterlife. What was it, then? She decided to investigate.

She stood still and listened for a moment. The sound was coming from a cellar door a little way off to her left. She put her hand on the latch and heard it click open, and she pulled at the door. The sound of a dog in distress got louder. Emily peered in. The cellar space was vast. Clearly it was currently being used as a storage space for all the gaudy accoutrements of the performers at the house because she could see, stacked in the shadows, eight giant painted heads and other objects whose form and function was less discernible. Half a dozen fireworks exploded in the sky above her, and a little of the light reached down into the darkness and showed Emily a few bars of what seemed like a cage, and she heard the animal whimper again. What sort of brute would do something like this?

'Don't open it!' A man's voice. She turned. It was Chris.

'There's a dog down there – I can hear it whimpering.'

'So you thought you'd interfere? You didn't think it might have been put down there on purpose?'

'Yes, but seriously, why would anyone shut a dog down there in a cage in the darkness on a night like tonight?'

'You're a clever girl, Emily,' he said. 'You'll figure it out.'

He went past her – he didn't push, exactly, but he moved with intention, so that she had to step out of his way – and opened the door and went down into the cellar. Emily stood there for a moment, wondering what to do next. Then she saw Joe walking towards her out of the darkness. There seemed to be a rule tonight, that when she saw one of these two men, she'd shortly afterwards see the other – as if one always needed to be at hand to cancel the other's actions out.

'He's got a dog in there,' Emily said.

'Who? Chris?'

'You *knew* about it?'

'What can I do? He's the chief.'

'Oh my God!'

'It's one night only, Emily. It's OK.'

'It's really not.'

'Come. We can go into the house this way. Maybe you can have a drink.'

Joe walked further up the side of the house, and Emily followed him. It was very dark there. There was no path, and the only light was from the stars, the occasional firework, and whatever faint illumination reached them from the windows of the house higher up on the first and second floor. Emily stumbled and scratched her leg on some holly leaves and cursed, and Joe took her hand, matter-of-factly, so she wouldn't fall into the next bush.

She strained her eyes looking into the darkness. Was there someone else here? Up ahead of them, she heard the rustling sound of movement in the bushes. Or maybe it was the wind, or water in a stream. She thought she saw the glint of something silver – a knife? Or a bit of tinsel on a tree? She wanted to say to Joe that being in the dark was like being deep underwater, not being able to hear or turn round quickly enough to see the predator behind you. But then she scratched her leg again, and she hissed because it hurt, and then Joe stopped, so she stopped right behind him and listened to him breathing, and she didn't say anything about being underwater or what she thought she had seen.

He opened a door at the side of the house and led her into a corridor that smelled of damp stone. It was completely dark. The blackness in here trumped the blackness outside, which at least had layers and shapes in it. Joe edged forward, and Emily could tell from the way his left arm was moving that he was feeling for something in front of him – a doorway or a light. She put her hand lightly on his back and edged forward with him. 'Shh,' he said, though she hadn't said a word.

He must have reached what he'd been looking for because he stopped. A little bit of light appeared in front of them, and she could see that he had pulled at the edge of a very thick, heavy curtain until there was enough of a gap for him to peep round.

'Ach,' he said, very quietly. 'No, we're too late.'

'What is it?'

'The knife throwing.'

'We've missed it?'

'No, they're just about to start.'

'Well, can I see?'

'I suppose so. OK.'

She crouched, and he stood next to her, and they peeped through the gap in the velvet curtain like Victorian children on Christmas Eve. The sensation of standing next to him, spying on events in the grand hall, was both illicit and innocent. But just standing next to him in the darkness would have been very pleasant anyway.

The two sisters came in, to the sound of applause. 'Ah,' said Joe. And when Emily asked him, he bent down and whispered to tell her that this one was Zizi, this one was Zsa-Zsa. Apparently they were very well known; apparently they were from a famous knife-throwing family in Hungary, so Joe said, though Emily had never heard of them.

They were in their blue-grey spangly costumes, and finally Emily realised what the colour reminded her of – sharks. They were blindfolded with big, silky pale green scarves tied around their eyes. They looked vulnerable, bringing to mind the painting of *Hope* by George Frederic Watts that had hung in Emily's Nana's living room until she died, and they stood facing each other with their backs against opposite walls in a slightly recessed area of the hall that provided a natural stage. They were very close to where Emily and Joe were standing – a little too close, perhaps, if one didn't have faith in their aim – but they were a decent way away from their audience. Emily wondered if she should be worried that Joe had sounded so disappointed that he wouldn't be able to get them into the grand hall and over to the other side, and safety, before the act began.

The two sisters began to throw their ornate-handled knives simultaneously. The knives crossed mid-flight and stuck into the walls behind them, no more than two hands' width from where each sister stood. There was a pause, and then they threw again.

And again, delineating an unflattering larger version of their own shapes around themselves. It was really rather exciting, and there were gasps from the audience.

The two sisters looked identical. They both had blonde hair, red lipstick, matching costumes – superficial dressing-up details that made them look the same. Emily found it harder to see the difference between them than she had when she saw them off duty upstairs in the boudoir. Perhaps it was because their features were obscured by the blindfolds. Perhaps it was the way they threw their knives with precision, at exactly the same time.

Emily was just thinking, *You know, there's got to be more than skill involved in this; there's got to be some trick; there must be some safeguard to ensure they don't hurt each other...* And then something terrible happened – one of the knives hit Zsa-Zsa in the chest. She gurgled and slumped. Her blindfold slipped. She looked towards Emily beseechingly, it seemed – although it must have been Emily's imagination because Zsa-Zsa couldn't have known Emily was there. And then she died.

Some part of Emily's brain was saying to her, *Look, don't be so unsophisticated. Just wait a few moments; this is all part of the act. This girl is going to get up and bow, and everything's going to be all right.* But people in the audience were screaming, some had started running towards the girls. The people who were furthest away, who couldn't see what had happened and who could only hear the confusion and the screaming, they reacted as though everyone in that hall must be in danger from some as yet unnamed thing – a fire, a flood, a terrorist cabal – and they started running away.

While all this was going on, the guests who were still enjoying the party in the garden outside, who either didn't want to see the knife-throwing act or who couldn't get in because it was too crowded, they were carrying on as normal; they were laughing, singing. The sound outside seemed to come in waves, as if someone was throwing it in dollops at the walls and trying to make it stick. It provided a rather sinister soundscape.

Joe had run forward towards Zsa-Zsa. Emily ran forward too, reaching for her phone. Others had got their phones out before her; others were calling the police, dialling 999. Joe was kneeling next to Zsa-Zsa, motioning at the crowd to keep back. Other performers had linked arms in front of the crowd –

she saw Elise there in her belted raincoat, and the Vie en Rose people – and they were doing their best to keep order and keep everyone back, including Emily's neighbour Victoria, the mother of the skate-boarding children, who was standing there with a very non-plussed expression, arms folded, head slightly tilted to one side.

And then Emily saw something – a clue! The knife that had stuck in Zsa-Zsa's chest was not one of the ornate daggers Emily had seen upstairs in the boudoir. It was an ordinary long-handled kitchen knife. Emily looked around and above her. There were people hanging from the balconies above to look at what was going on. There were two staircases leading down into this grand hall. Anyone could have thrown that knife.

The police arrived, their radios yapping – in Brixton, you're never more than two minutes away from a squad car full of Her Majesty's finest. The place was in chaos. Behind her, Emily saw Joe dragging Zsa-Zsa away, out into the corridor where he and Emily had come in, leaving a trail of blood on the floor. Emily would have liked to intervene to tell him they didn't do it like that on TV. Shouldn't he respect the crime scene? But she felt she should get to the police and offer herself as a witness. She had been close enough to see every detail and sober enough to remember what she had seen. Even as she approached the police officers, she tried to think about what she had noticed and press it down hard into her brain, in case some little nugget of information that she laid bare turned out to be important in their enquiry. She went over it and over it like a teenager cramming for her exams: the knife was an ordinary long-handled knife, the blindfold slipped, I saw the light go out of her eyes.

'A murder has taken place!' someone announced grandly, as if they were playing the butler at a themed dinner party. At least it wouldn't be difficult to solve: there were so many, many witnesses. Though possibly none was so reliable as Emily. If she could only reach the police... She had almost got there when there was a huge burst of applause. People were grinning, looking back towards the place where Zsa-Zsa had died. Emily looked, too, and was astonished at what she saw: Zizi and Zsa-Zsa had turned up again. Zsa-Zsa had apparently died, and yet she was standing there right as rain in her bloodstained costume with the knife still sticking out of her chest. She pulled it from her costume and waved the silly stubby thing at the audience. She smiled, a strange sly smile. It was just a prop. She and her sister held hands and bowed at the audience and bowed to each other, and everyone gasped and was astonished and then clapped.

Emily looked back towards the velvet curtain, and Joe was standing there clapping vigorously, smiling away and nodding. Suddenly he didn't look so attractive, with his head wagging clownishly up and down on his neck. Emily looked towards the police officers and saw Chris talking to them. She couldn't hear what he was saying, but she could read his body language, the apology as his hands went up and he shrugged and told them the audience reaction to a performance had got out of hand.

The police officers were responding to a call on a night when every firework functions like a trick or treat for them because it sounds like a gunshot. They were busy, modern local police officers in bulletproof vests, not the tweedy Scotland Yard detectives who traditionally turn up in murder mystery stories. Nor were they career detectives in the middle of nowhere, who desperately needed this to be the murder investigation that would make their name. They were in London, soon enough there would be another stabbing. They didn't look amused, they didn't look disappointed, they didn't look as though they were going to arrest everyone for wasting police time. But elsewhere in London there were murders and knife crimes and silly children setting off fireworks – all sorts of things that had to be investigated on a very busy weekend – and they were obviously keen to leave.

So this was just another performance – a special Halloween performance for the party-goers from their new friends at the bottom of the street. It had been a fantastic theatrical trick. And yet... and yet... Emily was not so sure. She'd looked at Zsa-Zsa, and she'd watched as the light went out of her eyes. Emily had only just seen her dog die about a week before. That was the first time she'd ever seen a fellow creature die – and now it had happened again. And it was the same: Emily was sure Zsa-Zsa had died. Still, there she was, smiling and bowing.

Emily had an idea that the trick that had been performed was nastier than the one the audience thought they had seen. There were a few things that had been a little 'off' tonight. There was Zizi's rudeness in the boudoir before the performance, for example, when she had shut the door in Emily's face.

But did it really amount to suspicious behaviour, or was it pre-performance nerves, a knife-thrower's right to privacy? Emily would have liked to ask Midori's opinion, but her friend was at home, sleeping off the ill effects of that glass of punch. Could Midori have been put out of the way because she had seen something in that boudoir? Had someone slipped poison into Midori's punch? If so, who? Chris had offered her a glass of punch, but so had Joe. Anyone could have put their hand over Midori's cup while she sucked on those prawns, and dropped something nasty into it.

Emily decided to talk to Dr. Muriel and find out what Dr. Muriel made of it; she seemed like a very sensible witness-type person who could help to evaluate the facts. She wanted to talk to Joe about it. He had been standing next to her; he had dragged the 'dead' girl out of the grand hall and seen her come to life again. If it was only a trick, he'd be able to explain how it was done. Before she could talk to either of them, she had to deal with Chris. As she made her way across the grand hall, he intercepted her.

'Some trick, huh?' Chris said. 'Had me going.'

'You didn't know they were going to do it?'

'They like to keep me on my toes, those Hungarians.'

'They're Hungarian? Like Joe.'

'The name kind of gives it away: Zsa-Zsa.'

'It could be a stage name, like Midori choosing "Hana-bi".'

Chris made his funny face again. 'Midori's the name of a bright green melon liqueur. Did you know that? "DJ Melon". It's got quite a ring to it. It's half the reason I booked her for this evening, and then she told me she was going to go by "Hana-bi".'

'Chris, where's Zsa-Zsa? I need to talk to her.'

'She's around here somewhere.'

'Or Zizi – where could I find Zizi?'

'They're off duty now, Emily. I don't know. Maybe they're in one of the private rooms upstairs. Maybe they've gone to the pub.'

'Private rooms?'

'Even performers need privacy.'

Emily was going to ask him – she was going to *interrogate* him, to find out whether Midori had been poisoned for stumbling unwittingly on some secret – but Victoria came up and intervened. Victoria said, 'I heard the DJ got shot. She went down mid-set. That's what the boys said. Was she really hurt, or was it part of the act?'

Chris said, 'She got food poisoning. Apparently.'

'What we saw just now, though,' Emily said. 'The knife throwing. Was that really just an act?'

'What do you mean?' said Chris. He looked tired.

'Well, I looked at Zsa-Zsa,' said Emily, 'and her blindfold slipped after the knife went into her chest, and she looked at me, and the light went out of her eyes.'

'Really?' said Chris.

'Really!' said Victoria.

'Yes,' said Emily. 'It reminded me of when my dog died.'

Chris looked at her for a moment or two. Emily thought that perhaps he was thinking of their altercation by the cellar door and was quaking a little, taking her seriously now as a dog owner who wouldn't stand for the ill-treatment of a dog in his care. Or perhaps he was wondering if it was too late to call the police back to investigate now that Emily had come forward as a witness to tell him what she had seen. She waited to see what he would say – it would be interesting to see if he could say anything without a note of exasperation in his voice. But no... he was about to speak, and unfortunately it seemed the words were to be accompanied by a sneer.

'Does the light really go out of a creature's eyes when it dies?' Chris said. 'Really? A fish that's been out of the river for a while, yes, it gets a milky look in the eyes and a slightly fishy smell. But it's not like the soul leaving the body and curling upwards like a wisp of smoke. The light is not "in" someone's eyes in the first place. Look, I'm sorry, Emily, because you're obviously overwrought because your dog has died. But the light going out of Zsa-Zsa's eyes – it's like something in a story.'

'Where is she, then?' said Emily. 'Zsa-Zsa?'

Chris looked irritated. He said, 'She's not here.'

'She can't have just disappeared!'

'There's no mystery about it, Emily. If she wanted a break from this place, all she had to do was walk to the main road and hop on a bus.'

'All right. But I'd like to talk to Zizi.'

Chris smiled politely enough. He walked off towards the staircase without answering. Emily wondered, was he heading to the first floor boudoir to warn Zizi that Emily was on to her?

Emily stood in the middle of the grand hall and came to a decision. Yes, OK, maybe the light didn't go out of Jessie's eyes. Another way of putting it would be to say that she had ceased to be. But Zsa-Zsa had ceased to be, too – right in front of her. And dead people don't come back to life, so Emily was going to find out what was going on. Her first potential witness scurried past: Elise. She'd been standing at the front of the crowd while the knives were being thrown, and what's more, she'd be able to give Emily an insider's perspective on the relationship between Zsa-Zsa and Zizi.

'Elise!' called Emily.

Elise came over. She said, 'I need your help in a matter of the utmost importance.'

Emily said, 'I need your help, Elise. It's about the knife throwing. Can I ask you a few questions?'

Elise stood still and held up one finger. She looked at Emily. 'Could you help me get the suitcase to the gentleman?' she asked.

'Well...' said Emily.

'My name is Elise. I need to get a message to our friend, but I'm being watched. I have

49

information that is vital, *vital*, to the success of our joint endeavour.'

'What's the message?' asked Emily.

Elise looked surprised at the question. 'Why, the message is in the suitcase.'

'OK, then. Who's it for?'

'The message is for the gentleman who is waiting for it, of course.'

'But, Elise, seriously – if that is even your real name – it's very neat that you're answering in character, but this is really real. Zsa-Zsa was your friend, wasn't she? Don't you want to help her?'

Elise said, 'Actually, no one liked her.' She said it in the same breathy voice she used for everything.

Emily looked at her for a while, and then she said, 'If I help you get the suitcase to the man, will you answer a few of my questions?'

Elise brightened. She even looked grateful. She said in a very low voice, 'I have to get the suitcase to the gentleman by the end of the evening. If there's no one to help me, I have to keep on asking.'

'So,' said Emily, 'let me get this straight. Your performance ends when you get the suitcase to the

50

gentleman. And if I help you do that, you'll be off duty and maybe you'll answer some of my questions. OK, so where's the suitcase? Where's the gentleman?'

'The suitcase is in the nursery in the attic. The gentleman will be waiting down here, in the grand hall.'

'OK. I'll go up and get it. And what about him? Will I recognise him?'

'Yes,' said Elise. 'But be careful with the suitcase. The contents are very fragile.' Then she whirled off, very fast, running up the nearest of the two staircases in dainty dancer's shoes, presumably so she could prepare the suitcase, or at least spy on Emily to make sure she went up to the attic to keep her part of the bargain. Emily took the other staircase – why not – and headed up to the attic.

When she got to the first floor, she looked into the bedroom where she had first seen Zizi and Zsa-Zsa – how simple it would have been to have found them there and questioned them. But the place was empty. She went in and walked around; she went into the bathroom. What had Midori seen, if anything? Was it anything that someone would have poisoned her to keep her from repeating and spoiling their secret? Emily looked around the bedroom and saw only what she had seen the first time – the dressing table with the make-up and hairbrush. The bed. She looked into the cupboards and saw five identical blue-grey spangly costumes – some shabbier than others – and four pairs of matching shoes, and found that she approved that they had spares; it must make doing the laundry less stressful.

When she reached the attic, she found two doorways. One door was shut – she tried the handle, but it was locked. The other door stood open to reveal a small room in the eaves, with clean bare floorboards and an empty crib in the middle of the room. Next to it, she saw a large suitcase. It was brown leather with a metal trim. She took the handle and found that it was very heavy – she'd have been liable for an excess baggage charge if she'd tried to take it onto an aircraft, that's for sure. Before she tried to move the suitcase, she paused to take stock of her murder investigation. It was following rather a circuitous route. Still, perhaps Elise would have a useful clue. She was the only performer Emily could really talk to. Chris was sardonic and rude. Joe was...

Joe was possibly implicated in covering up whatever had happened. Yes, Elise was her best chance.

Emily dragged the suitcase across the wooden floor. The sound of the metal edges of the suitcase on the wooden floor was a loud groaning protest, as if she was trying to dig a wood sprite from the knots in the floorboards. After she had managed to move the case to the doorway, she rested. After this, all she had to do was get the suitcase along the corridor and down two flights of stairs and into the grand hall in front of various assembled neighbours – and bingo, she'd be there. She put her hands on the handle and strained again to move it. She got it level with the locked door of the room next to this one. The door opened, its occupant no doubt intrigued by the dreadful noise.

'Emily?' Chris was leaning in the doorway to a sparsely furnished bedroom, legs crossed, arms folded, smiling like a model on a knitting pattern. In spite of herself, Emily peered into the room to see whether he was hiding Zsa-Zsa or Zizi in there, dead or alive. She saw a single mattress on the floor, made up comfortably with clean white sheets, a beige blanket and two fat pillows on it. She saw a straight-backed dining room chair with a pair of men's trousers and a pale blue T-shirt slung over it; a laptop computer on a very small table; and next to it, a lipstick in a gold case. The room was purely functional, a cell to sleep in – a cell for Chris to sleep in – not part of the performance space.

Chris said, 'At last! A volunteer. You're plucky, taking on the task yourself. It's heavy, isn't it? You want me to help you?'

'No, thank you,' said Emily with great dignity. When she was at school, it had always been implied that heavy lifting should be avoided because it might damage a woman's uterus. Now she hoped that if she came to grief from ignoring this advice, and the blasted thing shot out of her as she heaved at the suitcase, that at least it might land on Chris's head and choke him, mythical giant squid-like, with fallopian tentacles.

Chris smiled. He locked the bedroom door behind him and walked off down the stairs.

'Ems?' Now here was Victoria just behind Emily, doing her quizzical owl-head pose and standing in the way. 'Why don't you leave that for one of the men?'

'No, well. You see, it's a kind of performance.'

'Ooh! How clever. So it's not really heavy?'

'Well, no. It is really heavy. But I said I'd get this suitcase downstairs for Elise. The one in the raincoat?'

Fair play to Victoria, she bent down and tried to help. With both of them tugging on the handle of the suitcase, they made some progress down the corridor till they reached the top of the staircase – but it was slow.

Why don't you get your hateful progeny to help? thought Emily.

'You know what?' said Victoria. 'Why don't we get the boys to help?' She put two fingers in her mouth and whistled. Then she shouted, 'Tommy! Jolyon! Kim!' With names like that, presumably she was hoping to get the whole bunch of them into Parliament.

'It's a question of physics,' said Emily as the boys appeared. 'Or is it geometry? Angles and levers and–'

'Why don't we just push it down the stairs?' said the middle one, Jolyon. 'Let gravity do the rest. That's physics.' He put his hands on the upturned edge of the suitcase.

'No!' said Emily. 'The contents are fragile. I have to get the suitcase to a gentleman. It's a matter of *vital importance*.'

'Yeah,' said Kim from behind his wolf mask. 'She told us that 'n' all. You know it's only a game?'

'If we put the boys in the front as buffers,' said Victoria, 'and we hold on for dear life behind...' She motioned Jolyon and Kim to take up position and looked round for the third of her buffers, and there he was, skateboarding along the corridor in his habitual insolent pre-teen boy way.

'Well, with the skateboard,' said Emily. 'We can improvise.'

They put the skateboard, wheels up, on the banister. They laid the suitcase on the skateboard, using it like a tray. They held on and slid the thing down two flights of stairs, then they flipped the skateboard over and used it like a dolly to get the suitcase to the gentleman in the grand hall.

Emily was very grateful for the assistance of Victoria and her sons – she couldn't have done it without them – but still, it had been a tougher job than she'd bargained for when she accepted it, and she was sweating horribly by the time they arrived. She looked around for the 'gentleman', expecting to see the young man in the top hat with the rouged cheeks who had rushed past her when she first arrived at the party – or any kind of theatrical, dressed-up, amusing type. Anyone but Chris.

'Aha!' said Chris, when he saw her.

'I was looking for a gentleman,' said Emily, primly.

Chris said, 'Well, you'll have to make do with me.' He bent down and tapped at the suitcase, very gently, almost tenderly, as if its delivery really was a matter of vital importance. 'Shall I do the honours?' he said. 'Or will you?'

Emily shook her head. Really, she'd got the thing this far – why couldn't he open it? But he took a key from his pocket and handed it to her with a bow, and by then a small inquisitive crowd had gathered, so she had no choice but to smile and play her part.

She bent and put the key in the lock, Chris and Victoria and the boys arranged behind her, smiling, arms on shoulders like the Von Trapp family, and as she flipped open the lid of the suitcase, all of a sudden something lithe and large and unexpected reared up at her like a jack-in-a-box. It was Elise. She had removed her raincoat and contrived to fit her body into that suitcase – it wasn't *that* big – and had made the journey with them. She was wearing a lovely, slinky, silver 1930s dress with a tasselled fringe at the hem and at the bust. 'Thank you,' she said to Emily. She stepped over the edge of the suitcase, fitted a cigarette into a holder, lit it, and prepared to walk away.

'Wait!' said Emily. She really didn't want to go through her questions in front of Chris – but she did want an answer.

Elise knew what she wanted. She said to Emily, 'Do you know your Chekhov?'

'*The Seagull*?'

Emily had seen the same production of *The Seagull* at The Barbican in London three times in 2003. A friend of her boyfriend had had a small part in it. 'No.'

'*The Cherry Orchard*?'

Emily was not sure that she had seen *The Cherry Orchard*. She looked out in the direction of the garden and remembered the small orchard with its apple, pear and cherry trees. Perhaps it was somehow relevant? Zsa-Zsa was buried down there at the bottom of the garden under a cherry tree?

'No.'

Emily was getting uncomfortable. She saw the faces of one or two of her neighbours in the crowd – the young black man who was always repairing his car. The Indian woman with the disabled parking space and the herb garden at the front of her house. Emily hoped they would think it was part of the show. She said to Elise, 'You'll have to give me a clue.'

'You really don't know?' Elise gave Emily a look of such contempt. Then she walked away.

'Do you need me to help you?' asked Chris.

'I really don't,' said Emily. Then she walked away too.

'Don't miss the parade,' called Chris. 'We're burning a witch.'

Somebody laughed. Then behind her, she heard the small crowd break into polite applause. Someone whistled – the chap who was always repairing his car, perhaps. Emily didn't look back.

Emily wanted to find Joe. She went out into the garden and saw him standing there, tall and handsome, easy to spot in the crowd. She went towards him as quickly as she could. Joe and Emily. With their very English names they could have been toddlers playing up while their mothers had a natter in Starbucks, except that Joe was so tall and so handsome and so Hungarian, and Emily was... Emily was sweating like an adult woman who has just lugged a suitcase containing a contortionist down two flights of stairs.

'That was mad,' she said. She meant the knife throwing, but she could have been talking about any of it.

Joe smiled, as though it was a compliment. 'They've lit the bonfire,' he said. 'Come and sit over here, or you'll smell as though you're forged in a volcano.' He took her hand and led her over to one of the wooden benches. They sat there for a moment. Joe seemed as exhausted as if he had personally raised Zsa-Zsa from the dead. If only that was a legitimate possible explanation. Emily looked around at the other guests in the garden, trying to decide what she wanted to ask him. Was she really going to ask him if he had just covered up a death? Perhaps the knife had slipped, and out of loyalty...

'Wait here,' Joe said. She must have looked as though she hadn't said what she'd come out here to say because he put his hand on her shoulder and said, 'I won't be long. I'll come back.'

'Do you know your Chekhov?' said Emily.

'What can you mean?'

'It's something Elise said. It's about Zsa-Zsa. I need to know the names of the plays.'

Maybe he looked at her strangely, and maybe he didn't. It was hard to see in the darkness with the smoke from the bonfire blowing in their eyes.

'No,' he said. 'I don't know anything.' He walked away.

Emily sat and waited. Not far from where she was sitting, the little stall was still going, serving roast pig straight from the spit. Emily spotted a very elderly lady she knew heading for the front of the long queue of people waiting to be served with a slice of pork. Emily only knew this lady as 'Auntie'. It was a term of respect rather than an acknowledgement of familial ties because Auntie was originally from Jamaica and Emily had never even been there on holiday. Auntie was small, but she was mighty. She was fierce. She stood in her slippers at the gate post in front of her house most days and greeted the world as it passed by. The gate post was only a few feet from her front window, so there was no doubt that she stood there not because she'd get a better view but because she wanted to hail the passersby and get a greeting in return.

Seeing the long queue for the roast pork, rather than wasting time trying to evaluate how long it would take her to wait and whether or not she should stand in line or come back, Auntie had taken the sensible decision to press her suit as one of the oldest people there and had walked to the front and held out her plate.

'Hello, Auntie,' Emily called.

Auntie gave a queenly wave, but she didn't look back. She was concentrating on her plate as the meat piled up on it. 'A liccle more,' she said to the man in the chef's hat each time he paused. 'A liccle more.'

Now Dr. Muriel was heading in Emily's direction, her cane in one hand, a cup of punch in the other. 'I wonder if it's true,' Emily said to her, 'that roast pork smells like roasting human flesh.'

She'd thought Dr. Muriel would say something obvious like, 'Let's hope we never find out!' Instead she said, 'When is something "true", Emily? Is it when you read about it or hear about it, when you see it with your own eyes – or is there some other term of reference for you?'

'In this case,' said Emily. 'I'd have to smell it with my own nose, wouldn't I?'

Dr. Muriel sat down next to Emily, as though Emily had been waiting for her. So Emily took advantage of the situation to expound her theories about the knife throwing.

'No one has seen Zsa-Zsa since the knife throwing. Did she die right in front of me? Was she stabbed afterwards? Or is she alive?'

'It might have been an accident,' said Dr. Muriel. 'Seems like a night for mishaps. A girl just set herself on fire over there by the house. One of the performers. A silly girl with a cigarette holder and a silver flapper dress. The fringe of her dress went up, whoosh! Luckily for her your friend whatshisname, Sonny Jim, he was there to smother the flames.'

Was he? Emily thought of Joe, heroic and strong, wrestling Elise to the ground to save her from burning– and hopefully bruising her a bit in the process.

She said, 'It could have been anyone at the party who threw that knife.'

'But if Zsa-Zsa died, then who was it who came back again to show us that it was a prop? To show us that she *hadn't* been killed with a knife? You're not saying they did something with mirrors?

Or videotape? I was watching, and I saw that girl come back, large as life.'

'So we have suspects,' Dr. Muriel said. 'But no murder. That's interesting. That's a conundrum. "Remember, remember, the 5th of November. Gunpowder, treason and plot." How very apt that you should be investigating a murder that may not have happened, on Bonfire Night, a night which celebrates a regicide that never happened. You need a motive, don't you? Though before you start with that, I'd say you need to have a murder.'

'I've got a murder – I've just got to convince everyone else.'

'All right then, m'dear. You need a body. If there's been a murder, there will be a body.'

'You're right. I need to find one. And if I can't find one, I can at least look.'

'Flower beds? Anything recently dug up.'

'It's just a tangle of weeds everywhere. Nothing has been touched for twenty years.'

'The bonfire? You couldn't really tuck a body in there without the whole lot falling down like a pile of fiddlesticks.'

'Let me think.' Emily closed her eyes to concentrate, and instead of seeing where they might have hidden the body, she thought of Jessie. Even at the end, when everything else had gone – sight, hearing, back legs and sphincter – Jessie could smell a gravy bone across the kitchen. She'd have enjoyed the game of hunting for Zsa-Zsa, even if it was rather a ghoulish game. And as Emily thought of Jessie, it was almost as though the dog was helping her with her enquiries (only almost because, of course, she didn't believe in ghosts), and she thought about that cellar with the poor dog in a cage down there. A dark cellar would be a very good place to hide a body.

She opened her eyes and looked towards the side of the house where the cellar was situated. She could see Joe arguing with Chris and Zizi up by the locked side door to the house where Midori had vomited.

'I feel that I'm going about this the wrong way,' Emily said to Dr. Muriel. 'I should just ask Joe. Or Zizi. Or any of them. I should ask them straight out.'

'Indeed,' said Dr. Muriel. 'But you won't know what to ask them unless you find a body. If it was just a jolly good trick, they won't tell you their professional secrets, will they?'

'If there's been a murder, I don't suppose they'll confess. Who'd want to admit to killing someone?'

'You'd be surprised,' said Dr. Muriel. 'There are boastful people, frightened people, and those who just want to unburden themselves. You know, in my line of work, I enquire into all sorts of tricky situations, and after a while, one starts to see that there is no absolute right and wrong. There is only what might be and what must be. One quickly adjusts to the idea that in certain situations, for certain people, it would be no trouble at all to kill someone.'

Emily stood and looked down for a moment on Dr. Muriel's meaty-looking shoulders and that cane with the silver head on it. 'Assuming that's not a confession,' she said, 'I'll go and look in the cellar. Unless you want to save me the trouble and tell me where you hid the body?'

Dr. Muriel laughed and waved her cane. Emily set off towards the cellar – and Joe.

'Was that Zizi you were talking to?' she asked Joe. There was no sign of Chris or Zizi. Or Zsa-Zsa.

'She's not very happy with me,' he said. He looked embarrassed.

'I'm going to the cellar, Joe. I think Zsa-Zsa may be in there.'

'Really? You think Chris locked her in there with that dog? He's not such a bad man as you make out.'

'I saw the three of you arguing. I wish I could talk to Zizi.'

'She's leaving,' said Joe. 'Maybe she already left.'

'Just Zizi?'

'They're leaving. Isn't that what I said? Their mother is sick in Hungary. She has Alzheimer's. They have to go back.'

'The thing is, Joe...' How to put this? 'I really want to know what happened tonight. You dragged a dead body out of there after the knife throwing. And then, miraculously, she seemed to come to life.'

'What you talking about, Emily?'

'I told you about my dog?'

'Emily, tonight you told everybody.'

'She was old, and I knew she was going to die. I was really worried about it. I hoped that she would die in her sleep. But she got more and more frail, and more and more old, and in the end I had to get the vet to come round. And it was actually a peaceful death – so much so that, in my emotional state, I felt that I could almost enjoy going round with the vet, from house to house, watching as animals are killed peacefully.' Emily was getting a bit off-track here. 'But of course, that sounds a bit weird. What I mean, Joe, is that I watched as she died. And she just ceased to be.'

Not surprisingly, Joe looked bemused. 'I'm sorry about your dog, Emily.'

'I watched and saw exactly the same thing with Zsa-Zsa. I know she died. So what happened? Was it an accident? Did Zizi throw inaccurately? Did someone throw a kitchen knife from the balcony?'

'It was a stunt, Emily. But Zizi threw a bit hard. Her sister fainted. I pinched her ears in the corridor, and she stood up and took her bow.'

'You pinched her ears?'

Joe smiled. He leaned forward and took hold of the outer edge of her left ear with his right hand. He didn't pinch it. He touched her, and then he let go. 'Try it,' he said. 'It really works. You know?'

'Zsa-Zsa fainted?'

'It was a bit emotional. They had a row today.'

'Ah. I thought so.'

'They look identical. When a man's tired... When a man's tired and a girl gets into bed with him... Maybe the sister plays a trick, and it gets out of hand.'

'Chris! The weasel! I saw that lipstick in his bedroom. I can't believe I missed such an obvious clue. He slept with both of them? No wonder they were angry.'

'Emily, maybe it's not the man's fault.'

'It's always the man's fault, Joe. So Zizi killed her? She stabbed her sister out of jealousy? I'd been trying to find a motive – people smuggling, drugs, diamonds...'

Joe had been looking worried but he laughed at Emily's list. 'Emily, nothing happened. There wasn't a murder.'

'I saw it happen.'

'I know you feel sad about your dog. Everything doesn't relate back to that. You know?'

'And Chris is implicated. I know you're covering up for them, but you'll get in trouble if you don't go to the police, Joe.'

'But somebody already called the police – they came here and saw for themselves there wasn't a murder.'

'Yes. That's the clever bit. Now if we call again and tell them what happened, they'll never believe us. We need evidence. All I have is theories, but I *know* Chris put something in Midori's drink and poisoned her. He set fire to Elise because she tried to give me a clue.'

'Chris set fire to Elise?'

'Dr. Muriel told me. Her dress caught fire, and Chris was there. I thought she was talking about you, but she meant Chris. Setting fire to someone or smothering the flames – to an onlooker, there's very little difference. He was giving Elise a warning, telling her to keep silent. He's dangerous, Joe. You be careful.'

'Emily, I tell you what. I think you're crazy, but I'll talk to Chris. I'll talk to Zizi. I'll see if I can find Zsa-Zsa. Will that do?'

But Emily was distracted. Up ahead in the darkness, near the house, she could just about make out Dr. Muriel skirting past the bushes. She was heading for the cellar. 'You see what you can find out,' Emily said to Joe. 'I'm sorry. I've got to go.'

Before Emily could reach her, Dr. Muriel had opened the cellar door and gone inside. Emily followed, hating the darkness. This was the king of darkness compared to the ill-lit passageway that led here and the corridor that looked on to the grand hall. This was a spidery darkness, full of stacked things and shadows – and, presumably, Dr. Muriel.

'Emily?' Dr. Muriel's voice was behind her. A light flared in the cellar, showing the row of giant faces painted on fibreglass heads as big as a person, each one with different features, but similar in construction to the glowing heads Emily had seen in the garden when she first arrived. She looked for the cage with the dog in it, but it had gone.

'Dr. Muriel?' Emily called. 'Is it just you in here?'

'Come and look at this, m'dear.'

Emily went back towards the cellar door. She saw a thin beam of light from a pen torch on a key ring as Dr. Muriel shone it on a painted sarcophagus, depicting a larger than life-size pink naked woman with long black hair and big blue eyes, her nudity innocent as a mermaid's, though from what Emily could see of it, she had legs. Dr. Muriel tapped, like an electrician tapping at panelling to check whether the space behind it is hollow and might contain wires that could kill if someone drills into them. She pulled at a catch on the side of the lady, just about where her ribs would be, and lifted the lid upwards to reveal another painted lady inside. It was Zsa-Zsa, the kitchen knife still in her chest, her pretty face tinged with a blue that matched her costume.

'I know what you said about right and wrong,' Emily said. 'But until you see something like this, you can't really believe it.'

Dr. Muriel said, 'Sometimes people are driven to do terrible things.'

And then, as if proof were needed – which it was not – Emily felt the business end of Dr. Muriel's cane on the back of her head, and she went down in a lump.

A short while later, Emily regained consciousness. She was standing upright, and her legs were untethered, but her arms were pinioned. She was in darkness, her upper body enclosed in a roughly spherical space. The air that she breathed had the smell of an art room about it. From outside, roast pork and bonfire smokiness drifted into the cellar – she couldn't have been unconscious for too long. It was still the night of the party.

'Emily,' called Dr. Muriel, fairly robustly, considering the circumstances, 'what is this? A pantomime horse.'

'I think you might be inside a giant head. You didn't whack me, did you, with your cane?'

'No, of course not! You really are a most suspicious girl.'

'Dr. M., what do you know about Chekov?'

'Ah, well.' Dr. M cleared her throat as if to start on a very long lecture. Her voice echoed slightly in her improvised prison. 'The Russians, of course–'

'I mean, tell me the name of some Chekov plays.'

'*The Seagull.* I think that might be my favourite because–'

'Dr. Muriel, can you just give me a list?'

'*The Seagull, The Cherry Orchard, Uncle Vanya...* I could tell you a rather amusing story about the time I saw *Uncle Vanya* in–'

'Please don't.'

'*Three Sisters.*'

So that was it. '*Three sisters!*' Emily said. 'It seems obvious now, doesn't it? It's simple arithmetic. If two are alive and one is dead...'

An arc of light swung through the darkness in the cellar – Emily could see it through the peepholes in the head, which were located in the nostrils that had been painted on the face. She looked for the painted sarcophagus, but she couldn't see it. She couldn't see who was in the cellar with them – whether rescuer or assailant. 'Shh,' she whispered to Dr. Muriel. 'I think we're not alone.'

'What's that, m'dear? SPEAK UP!' said Dr. Muriel.

The light swung again. This time Emily had a chance to see who was there – it was Chris. He held a powerful torch, which he put on the ground in front of him. Now he was standing just in front of her with an axe in his hand. Emily tried to determine whether she should run for her life (and look ridiculous) or stay still or aim a good kick at him and hope he didn't chop her legs off.

'Emily!' said Chris. 'Nice head. Is this going to be another performance?'

She said, 'Don't do anything stupid, Chris. The police know I'm here.'

'Of course they do.' He came up very close, his eye to her peephole.

'Chris!' shouted Dr. Muriel from inside her giant head. 'Is that you?'

Chris turned at the sound of Dr. Muriel's voice and swung his axe violently.

'No!' screamed Emily. She shut her eyes in spite of herself. She opened them again to see through the nostril peepholes that he was coming for her now. He swung his axe. The fibreglass prison split open. She stepped free; she was unharmed. She looked to her left, and Dr. Muriel was there, also unharmed. Their well-being seemed to provide yet another clue to the case, which Emily tried to process.

Chris took Emily's hand and pulled her towards him. He looked as if he was going to hug her.

'Where's the dog that was down here?' asked Emily.

'My dog? Sam. He was frightened of the fireworks, so I put him down here out of the way. Honestly, Emily, he lives like a prince the rest of the time. It was for one night, and it was for his own good. But OK, you made me feel guilty, so I put him up in my room.'

'Where's that sarcophagus?' said Dr. Muriel. 'The painted lady? Zsa-Zsa's in it.'

'If you mean the witch that was in here, she's part of the parade. They're going to put her on the bonfire and burn her. Seriously, you think Zsa-Zsa's in it? It's supposed to be empty.'

Dr. Muriel said, 'Chris, we know she's in it. We've seen her.'

They scrambled out of the cellar. Out in the garden, the parade had already started. It was an ethereally beautiful sight: A procession of six giant heads lit from inside seemed to float towards the bonfire, flanked by eight Polish stilt-walkers in top hats and coattails, juggling flaming torches. It all looked desperately dangerous – but these people were about to burn (albeit unwittingly) the body of a young woman who had been murdered a few hours before, so it seemed ridiculous to cavil about Health and Safety.

At the front of the procession, Emily saw the sarcophagus being carried on the shoulders of a couple of men. The distance between the house and the bonfire wasn't that great, but the performers were making the most of it by covering the width as well as the length of the garden, winding from one side of it to the other very slowly, weaving around the fruit trees in the orchard. Now they were heading back. The garden was packed with spectators. Some stood on the wooden benches and applauded; others surrounded the performers, pressing in to get a good look. A few – the kids, mostly –joined the back of the parade.

'Stop!' yelled Chris. But the music was too loud. Nobody heard him

'But who knocked us out in the cellar?' Dr. Muriel asked Chris as they pressed through the crowd towards the bonfire. 'And why didn't the performers notice us as they brought the heads out, or at least notice they were only bringing out six giant heads instead of eight of them for the parade?'

'The props guy was supervising.'

'Joe?' asked Emily.

'Yes, Joe.'

'Joe set this up?'

Chris said, 'I don't know if he set it up or he was covering up. He's pretty resourceful. I guess if he knew Zsa-Zsa was dead, he presumed the person who killed her was Zizi. He's in love with Zizi.'

Emily was slightly out of breath from the running and jostling. By now she and Chris were about halfway between the front and the back of the parade. They had left Dr. Muriel behind. Emily was panting as she said, 'Joe was involved with Zizi? But I saw her lipstick in your bedroom.'

'Did you? Boy, you're nosey. It must have been Zsa-Zsa's. The sisters weren't speaking to each other before the performance. I had to let Zsa-Zsa get ready upstairs in my room. For a while there we thought she wasn't even going to go on.'

'So the sister I saw in the boudoir was the third sister? No wonder they didn't look identical – just similar.'

Chris said, 'I don't know, Emily. You're the detective.'

The parade had reached the bonfire. People had begun chanting. 'Burn the witch! Burn the witch!' Chris and Emily had pushed their way to the front – Auntie would have been proud.

'Stop!' yelled Chris again. He and Emily leapt on the two men who were carrying Zsa-Zsa in her colourful coffin. As she wrapped her arms and legs around him to tackle him, Emily was sorry – but not surprised – to discover that one of the men was Joe.

As it was knocked to the ground, the lid of the sarcophagus sprang open, and there was Zsa-Zsa: bluish, beautiful, dead, with the knife in her chest.

'Call the police,' someone said. It might have been Emily.

Emily disengaged herself from Joe. After she and Chris had toppled him, she had lain, briefly, on top of Joe, her knees tucked up (but clasped demurely together) at about the level of his waist, her head tucked under his chin, her ear on his throat – like a very tired or frightened young monkey clinging for comfort to its mother.

'I'm sorry, Emily,' said Joe, as he stood up. A Polish stilt-walker grabbed his shoulders, and Ravi from Emily's local shop held on to his elbows. But Joe offered no resistance.

Dr. Muriel caught up with them, ploughing through the crowd with elbows and cane before her, giving a knock to anyone who didn't get out of the way. Emily turned her friend right round again and walked with her back to the house.

'So the third sister turned up in London last night and asked one of them or both of them to go back to Hungary with her to help with the sick mother?' said Dr. Muriel as they made their way through the scandalised crowd, which by now was buzzing with news of the discovery of Zsa-Zsa's body.

'It seems so. But there was an argument, and Zizi refused to leave Joe, so Zsa-Zsa set him up and got into bed with him so her sister would think they'd been sleeping together and get angry.'

'Well, certainly she got angry. That was quite a betrayal.'

'Yes. But the plan backfired, and Zizi refused even to let Zsa-Zsa get ready in the same bedroom, and Zsa-Zsa threatened that she wasn't going to perform. So Zizi put the third sister in one of the shabby spare costumes in case she had to go on.'

'A bit of a risk – if she was out of practice, we might have ended up with a different dead body.'

'They're from a famous knife-throwing family, apparently. Very well known in Hungary. Besides, I expect they could see through the blindfolds. Anyway, then... I don't know. Zsa-Zsa insisted on doing the performance, I suppose. And instead of using the sawn-off prop, Zizi threw a real kitchen knife and killed her.'

Dr. Muriel stopped and rested on her cane and looked up at the dark passageway that led past Midori's long-since-absorbed vomit puddle towards the side doors and the cellar. 'And the third sister was waiting outside in the bushes?'

'She must have been. You know, I thought I saw someone – or heard them. It was just a glinting and a bit of rustling. You know something else? When Zsa-Zsa died and she looked towards the curtain, she must have seen Joe. I thought she was looking beseechingly at me, but it must have been him. Maybe the light didn't go out of her eyes. But I know a beseeching look when I see one.'

'So Joe dragged Zsa-Zsa's body away from the grand hall, and the third sister stepped in to take the bow.'

'Yes. But whether she was in on it or she was just protecting Zizi, I have no way of knowing.'

'I suppose it will all come out in court,' said Dr. Muriel, sagely.

'One good thing about this evening,' said Emily. 'I didn't learn personally whether roast pig smells like a roast person.'

'And you let go of Jessie.'

'Hmm,' said Emily. 'Not quite.'

Chris caught up with them just before they reached the front door of the house. He must have been running because he looked flushed. He took Emily's hand, and he got a look on his face that made his nose seem longer and straighter than usual. Emily recognised it finally for what it was: shyness. It twisted his mouth so it looked kind of sexy.

He said, 'Would you consider joining us, Emily? You've got a lovely loud shrieking voice; you were very game with that suitcase. You're tenacious; you're good at remembering things. You'd be, you know, an asset.'

Emily looked at him and thought that this might be the offer that would help her, finally, to forget Jessie, to let go and move on from her old life. 'Thank you,' said Emily. 'But no.'

The flashing blue lights and the protesting 'not ME, not ME, not ME' sound of the sirens announced that the police had arrived and were parking up on the road outside. Chris left Emily, with a somewhat reluctant final squeeze of her hand, and went off to deal with them.

'I'll walk you back to your flat, dear,' said Dr. Muriel to Emily. 'If you don't mind stopping by the kitchen first so I can pick up my trolley.'

As they walked together back to the house, Dr. Muriel said, 'I don't suppose we shall ever discover whether Midori was poisoned — but for what it's worth, I very much doubt it. That girl was overexcited and wearing very constricting clothing, and she bolted her food from what you told me, and she drank that punch down straight. It sounds like what my mother would have called a giddy spell – she was a classic candidate. Other than that, Emily, is there any aspect of this case left unresolved?'

'Well, I did wonder,' said Emily, 'whether Joe *really* liked my cheesy potato bake that I brought.'

'I don't know about that, m'dear,' said Dr. Muriel. 'But if it's pertinent to the case, I'm sure it will come out in court.'

SHOWSTOPPERS

'Hello!' Emily called as she went into her flat on Friday evening, before the front door was fully closed behind her. She lived alone. Calling out was a deterrent strategy in case she had been followed home by an opportunistic thief. The thief was to assume, from hearing her cheery hello, that she lived with a tough, dangerous man or men who wouldn't stand for Emily being attacked on her doorstep or pushed inside and attacked there. It was a strategy that she no longer thought about or questioned, she just did it. It was one of many little survival tactics she had adopted since coming to live in London – but still, when she called out hello and got no answer, it always seemed, somehow, as if the silence was mocking her for living alone.

She picked up her mail from the doormat: a phone bill, a begging letter from a charity, a voucher for free delivery from a supermarket, and a letter addressed to her neighbour, Victoria. It wasn't unusual for Emily to get letters delivered to her that were meant for other residents of the street, as though the postmen at the local sorting office were conspiring to bring the community into closer contact with each other. She took the letter across the street to where Victoria lived in a three-storey red brick Edwardian terraced house with her husband and three sons. Emily Castles was a bright, clever young woman with a natural curiosity. When she walked anywhere she walked quickly, usually, and she looked up at her surroundings as if she expected to see something interesting at any minute. But today hadn't been a good day, and she looked down at the chewing gum-grey pavements without really seeing them, scuttling towards Victoria's house to avoid being seen as much as to avoid seeing anything. But Victoria opened the door to greet her before Emily could get away. Victoria was very slim, and she had naturally curly brown hair that fell to her shoulders in fat spirals. She was in her early-to-mid forties, Emily thought. Victoria rarely wore make-up unless it was a special occasion because she had lovely skin and even features, and she looked perfectly fine without it.

She was bare-faced now, as usual, though Emily couldn't help noticing she looked paler than usual, even a little drawn.

'Letter for you,' said Emily.

'Oh God, no!' said Victoria. 'Oh my God!' She put one hand to the base of her throat and reached for the door behind her with the other, as if planning on whipping it off its hinges and using it as a shield. Her reaction was unexpected to say the least. 'Come in, Ems,' she said. 'Please.'

Emily longed to get back home so she could spend the evening on the sofa with a packet of ginger biscuits and a nice cup of tea, watching rubbish on TV.

'Please!'

Emily followed Victoria into the lovely kitchen, where the family ate most of their meals. Everything was just so, in a country-living kind of a way: there was a range oven *and* a conventional oven; cupboards and units painted in forget-me-not blue; French windows opening onto the garden at the back; big wooden storage boxes for the boys' Wellington boots and trainers; and something deliciously Italian-smelling (herbs and tomatoes

 Helen Smith

and cheese in it or on it for sure, Emily thought)
cooking in the oven.

Emily put the letter on the big scrubbed pine
table. Victoria eyed it as though Emily had put a pet
snake there. 'Will you open it for me?' Victoria said.
'Only I think it might be bad news.'

Victoria and Emily weren't close. Victoria
was Emily's neighbour. Sometimes Emily looked in
and fed the cat and watered the plants when the
family was away. Sometimes she delivered letters to
their house that had been delivered to her by
mistake. If this letter contained bad news – a death
in the family? An estrangement? Foreclosure?
Bankruptcy? The expulsion of one of the boys from
school? – then Emily was hardly the right person to
open and read it and convey the news to Victoria.
She took a seat and leaned her elbows on the table.
She didn't pick up the letter.

'What about Piers? Can't he?'

'No!'

'But if it's bad news?'

'Not bad news so much as... danger.'

Victoria stood three feet away from the letter
with her arms folded, staring at it nervously. She
had a beautifully enunciated, ever-so-slightly-weary

voice that suggested she had been bred to have servants and marry the kind of man who, in previous generations, might have joined the army and ordered his social inferiors to charge in vain against a better-armed enemy. Actually she had learned to speak that way in elocution lessons. Even so, even if she *had* belonged to some ruling class, surely she was anchored securely enough in modern times to understand that if she thought the letter contained anthrax, she shouldn't be so selfish as to propose that Emily open the letter on her behalf and take the hit?

Emily looked at the letter, but she didn't move. Danger? She couldn't think what Victoria could possibly mean. She hadn't had a good day, and in her tiredness and bewilderment she felt as though she were the stupid one.

'Not that kind of danger,' said Victoria, reading Emily's expression. She came and sat down at the table without unfolding her arms, hooking a chair and drawing it back with one foot, all of which was quite a difficult manoeuvre, a bit like Russian Cossack dancing. Only when she was sitting opposite Emily did Victoria unfold her arms, putting her elbows on the table and clasping her hands together in prayer before Emily. Then she confessed.

'I've been getting nasty notes. Poison pen. I can't bear to look at it. Can you?'

'Maybe Piers...?'

'Piers mustn't know. Quick, Ems, he'll be home from work soon. Please! Please. Open it for me. You're a clever girl. You'll know what to do.'

It wasn't a question, Emily thought, of whether or not she'd know what to do, but whether or not she wanted to get involved. Victoria didn't seem to think that was up for consideration. She seemed to think that Emily would want to spend her Friday night opening and screening Victoria's mail, spending her free time doing unwaged what she'd normally do during working hours to make a living.

She opened the letter.

The following message was printed in capital letters in blue biro on pale blue notepaper, the kind of stationery that you might use to write a thank you note if you were seventy years old:

WHAT A DISGRACE
TO THE RED, WHITE AND BLUE

VICTORIA'S BEEN NAUGHTY
WHAT SHALL WE DO?

There was no address or signature.

'It's another one, isn't it?' said Victoria, watching Emily's expression.

'I don't know. What were the other ones like?' She handed Victoria the letter so she could see for herself.

'I'll rip it up and put it on the compost heap – the slugs and snails can choke on it.'

'You can't do that. It's evidence. If you're being threatened, or blackmailed... Are you being blackmailed?'

'"Evidence?" I can't go to the police. What about Piers's job?'

Piers was something important, Emily wasn't quite sure what, in the civil service. 'Victoria, what does it mean?'

Victoria said, 'It seems to imply, doesn't it, with the "red, white and blue" that they'll cause a scandal and Piers's job with the government will be at stake.'

'Where are the other notes? If someone's threatening you, you can't let them get away with it.'

Victoria brought her large, grey handbag over from where it had been squatting on the Welsh dresser, in front of the slightly dusty display of never-used blue-and-white crockery. She said, 'You know I used to be an actress?'

Yes. Everyone knew it. Victoria still had the cheekbones. She had done a bit of telly when she was younger, and popped up now and then in daytime repeats, in *Rumpole of the Bailey* or other dependable, once-popular British TV series. For whatever reason – love, Emily had always assumed – she had given it up, but now she ran a stage school locally, so the subject quite often came up, and even if people didn't watch much daytime TV, every one of her neighbours knew what she had once been.

'I made a video,' said Victoria. 'When I was a student...' She curled her fingers and put her hand up to her mouth and looked out of the window, her knuckles pressed against her lips as if to silence herself. Then she put her arms around herself and hugged tightly. Emily was impressed and slightly thrilled to be treated to this private performance of

Victoria playing 'woman for whom the memory of a youthful transgression is still painful'. She tried to think of a tactful way to say that no one would much care these days if a video of Victoria's bare bottom should show up on the Internet, unless she was really famous. The world was awash with pornography – Victoria's indiscretions would matter to no one but her.

'If it got onto the Internet,' said Victoria, 'I would be ruined.'

'It may not be as bad as you think,' said Emily. 'People these days are very broad-minded.'

'I'd say they're less broad-minded than they were twenty years ago. But that's hardly the point. Emily, a man died because of that video.' She stood, turned and did a press-lipped anguished face, and wrung her hands together. By now, all Emily's earlier cares had seeped away because she was so thoroughly absorbed by Victoria's elegant response to her troubles. Solo performances by actors of Victoria's calibre would do brilliantly well as part of executive redundancy packages, Emily reflected. If she were more entrepreneurial, she'd be off and making some phone calls about it now, setting up a new business. Instead, she said, 'A man died? Is that why you gave up acting?'

'God, no! The cost of child care in this country...'

'Besides, you've got Showstoppers now.'

'Not for much longer if these notes continue.' Victoria brought out two more notes from an inner pocket in her handbag and showed them to Emily. Like the one she had just opened, these contained sneering rhymes written on blue stationery.

> I KNOW VICTORIA'S SECRET
> I HOPE I CAN KEEP IT
> IF I SHOULD LEAK IT
> SHE WILL BE SORRY

And

> WHEN THEY KNOW WHAT I KNOW
> IT WILL STOP THE SHOW
> AT SHOWSTOPPERS

'Not exactly W H Auden, is it?' said Victoria. 'I can't show them to Piers. He did English at Oxford. He'd be mortified.'

'Has the sender made any demands for money?'

'Not yet.'

'It could be a bluff. Who else knows about the video?'

'I haven't told a living soul about it, Emily. The only people who knew about it were my boyfriend and me because we were in it. We filmed it ourselves. We didn't even hire a lighting guy.'

Emily was quiet for a while, thinking about what sort of person even considers hiring a lighting technician when filming *that* sort of video. Victoria watched her respectfully in her turn, as if Emily were mentally sifting through the evidence and would soon have a solution.

'Why would anyone send you something like that, Victoria?'

'I don't know *why*, but I know *who*. It's my old boyfriend, David. It has to be. I haven't seen him in twenty years or more, suddenly he turns up at the school. Next thing, I'm getting nasty notes through the mail.'

'He turned up at the school? What did he say?'

'I didn't talk to him. I just saw his name on the enrolment forms – he wants to get his daughter into Showstoppers. Or so he claims. I don't know if he even has a daughter.'

'You think he's stalking you? What does he want?'

'That's what we've got to find out.'

We? Emily had only popped across the road to deliver a letter. Suddenly she was being roped into investigating Victoria's possibly sordid relations with a possibly dangerous ex-boyfriend. And come to think of it, Victoria herself was possibly dangerous, too.

'You said someone had died?' said Emily.

But they were interrupted by the sound of the key in the lock, the front door opening, and then a hearty 'Hello!' in Piers's voice. Victoria half-rose from her chair and tucked the letters and envelopes into the back pocket of her jeans. As she sank back down again, she gave Emily a warning look.

'I think you should tell him,' whispered Emily. 'A secret's only really useful currency to a blackmailer when it remains a secret. Could there have been a mistake about the man who died? Maybe you're not responsible.'

'Oh yes! I hope so. That would be a weight off my mind after twenty years. But who do I ask? I can hardly go to the police.'

'Was it an accident? A car crash, something like that?'

Victoria listened for sounds of her husband outside, her head to one side, her finger on her lips. They heard Piers's footsteps in the corridor as he went about his normal just-back-home routine: hanging up his coat, finding a place for his laptop computer, washing his hands in the sink in the downstairs bathroom. In the long pause before she spoke, Emily thought again of Victoria's training as an actress – it was a very suspenseful pause. 'No,' said Victoria. 'He died laughing.'

Victoria was such a humourless person that Emily was impressed. She longed to know more, but there was no chance of it now.

'Hello, Emily,' said Piers, coming into the kitchen. 'Had a good week?'

'My contract came to an end today.'

'Oh, Emily,' said Victoria. 'I'm sorry. I didn't know. What a shame.'

'Bad luck!' said Piers.

'Oh, it's OK. It was only temporary anyway. Back to the agency on Monday.'

'Could you do some work at the school? Victoria always needs a hand there.'

'Yes!' said Victoria. 'Please do.'

'That's nice of you,' said Emily. 'But I need something long-term.'

'Oh, please! You'd be doing me a favour. I'm going to need help interviewing the new parents.' Victoria gave a 'special' look to Emily, but she needn't have bothered. Emily knew very well why Victoria wanted her at the school. Instead of getting a nice job at a proper office with a canteen, she was supposed to go and help out at Victoria's stage school and learn more, if that were possible, about her neighbour's life than she already knew – which was considerably more than she wanted to know.

Piers went to the fridge and opened a bottle of white wine. He got out three glasses, which was a good start. If you were thirsty, you could die from the want of a cup of tea or a glass of wine when Victoria was hosting. 'It would set my mind at rest to have a friend of Victoria's working there,' he said.

Emily wasn't friends with Victoria. Victoria sometimes gave her hand-me-down, very expensive, brightly-coloured twinsets. But friends? No.

'She gets very stressed when she's planning the end-of-term "extravaganza",' said Piers. 'Always threatens to close the school or flounce off and let someone else run it.' He filled a glass with wine and handed it to Victoria. 'I wish you would give it up, Vee. There are so many other things you could be doing if you didn't have the school – things we could be doing together.'

'I don't know why I do it: parents, patrons, prize-giving, tap-dancing, teenagers, toddlers, teachers' skits. *Stress*. And that's just the showcase. I'm also battling the landlord because he wants to sell up. The bills are sky-high. The infant toilets keep blocking up, and there's something wrong with the electrics that needs to be fixed by nine o'clock tomorrow morning. I'm *this close* to giving the place up and letting someone else run it. And now there's this other thing.'

'What other thing?' Piers asked.

'I could take you in and introduce you tomorrow,' said Victoria to Emily. 'We do weekends and after-school and school holidays, but tomorrow is our end-of-term showcase for the students at Showstoppers – it's a chance for them to put together everything they've learned – and we use it to recruit new students, too. Oh... I'll be OK when it's over and we go off on holiday. I love it, really. You'll love it, too. And the kids will love you. Do you dance?'

Emily said, 'No.'

'What other thing?' said Piers again.

Victoria looked at Emily, then she stood and took the poison pen letters from her back pocket and spread them out on the table.

'Crumbs!' said Piers. 'Not much of a poet, is she? Or he. Who's sending these, do you think?' He went and put his arm around Victoria's waist, glass of wine held at chin height in his other hand, and they stood together and looked at the notes as though they were at the private view of an art exhibition, trying to make sense of a perplexing exhibit.

'You remember I told you about David Devereux, my old boyfriend? We made a video together when we were students.'

'Did you?' Piers blushed, the pink patches on his cheeks girlishly endearing, as if he had put on a pair of pink fluffy slippers. 'I've never seen it.' He broke away from Victoria and sat down and drank a mouthful of his wine.

'Not that kind of video,' said Victoria. 'It was a performance piece for our degree. We began to wish we'd never made it. It brought everyone who watched it the most awful bad luck.' Victoria looked over towards the Welsh dresser. 'I don't even like to touch it, to be honest.'

'It's here?' said Piers. He went over to the dresser. It was obviously a dumping-ground for all sorts of once-useful or might-one-day-be-useful items. Piers crouched and opened the double doors at the bottom of the dresser and brought out: a ball of string, a cricket ball, an electric screwdriver – 'Oh! I've been looking for that!' – a roll of cellotape, a packet of plastic clothes pegs, four electric light bulbs... 'No,' he said, shovelling it all back in again. 'Can't see a video.'

'In the top drawer. With the pizza leaflets.' Victoria watched while Piers rummaged for a bit and then pulled an old VHS tape out of the drawer and brought it over to the table. She said, 'It was twenty years ago. I'd almost forgotten about it, but then it arrived in the post a week or so ago. The widow of my old tutor sent it to me. She's getting on a bit, and she's got to move into a care home. She found it when she was clearing out her house. There was a lovely note with it, saying, "I don't blame you for what happened to Bill."'

'Is the note anything like these ones?' asked Emily.

'No, unfortunately. Or fortunately. She was a really nice woman.'

'Why is it bad luck?' Piers asked.

'Well, David and I always believed that Bill – my old tutor – died because of it. And then we split up – though that's a good thing, in hindsight. Or I'd never have met you. It just seemed like one thing after another. Though death is much worse, of course, than the breakup of a love affair between two drama students.'

'He died because of your video?' said Piers. 'What on earth do you mean, Vee?'

'He had to evaluate it for our degree. It really was the most awful, earnest piece of tosh. An interpretive dance piece – we were very proud of it, of course, at the time. But we showed it to a few of the other students, and they cracked up laughing at it. My friend Gloria had an asthma attack – they had to take her to the walk-in health clinic and put her on the nebulizer. Then poor old Bill had a heart attack and died while he was watching it. They found him sitting in his arm chair in front of the TV, with this awful rictus grin.'

'Surely they didn't mention the awful rictus grin in the coroner's report?' said Piers.

'No. But that's what we heard afterwards from his wife – his widow. Everyone teased us, all the other students. They said he died laughing. I don't doubt it's true. Honestly, I can't bear to have it in the house. And now this business with the poison pen letters. What shall I do with the ghastly thing?'

'There's no such thing as bad luck brought by a video. Your tutor would have died anyway, Victoria, if he had a weak heart. You know that. You know what we ought to do? We'll watch it now – prove there's nothing in it.'

'Is it very long?' asked Emily. 'The video?'

'It's VHS,' said Victoria. 'We haven't got a machine that will play it in the house.'

103

'Have *you*, Emily?' asked Piers. He seemed ready for action.

Fortunately Emily only had a DVD player. But it seemed a good time to take her leave. 'I have some errands to run in the morning,' she said, meaning that she would like to stay in bed. 'But I could be at Showstoppers by ten o'clock tomorrow to help out.'

'That would be great!' said Victoria. Emily relaxed a bit – actually it might be quite nice to work for Victoria for a while. She smiled. The fragrant, delicious, very cold, expensive white wine that Piers had dispensed for her in a heavy, expensive wine glass had worked its magic on her. But then Victoria delivered her punch line, 'Unfortunately the children will start coming in around ten o'clock. It's best if I introduce you to the staff before that. Shall we say eight thirty-ish?'

The next morning, as she was on her way to Showstoppers shortly before ten o'clock (with Piers's help, she'd managed to talk Victoria into letting her have a later start), Emily saw her neighbour Dr. Muriel on the other side of the street. 'Lovely day for a wedding!' called Dr. Muriel, waving her stick in the air when she saw Emily. Dr. Muriel was a middle-aged feminist who lived alone. She was wearing a tweed skirt with a grass stain just above the hem, where she had knelt to weed her herbaceous border after cutting the lawn, going down on her right knee to do it like an old-fashioned suitor. Emily took a few moments to try to evaluate Dr. Muriel's comment. Given her appearance and her independent nature, Emily thought it unlikely that Dr. Muriel was on her way to a take part in a ceremony that would seal her future to that of a man or woman. Emily herself wasn't getting married. But it was a sunny day, and it was a Saturday, and someone, somewhere would be getting wed. Therefore she deduced that Dr. Muriel was just making a slightly obtuse remark that didn't merit a reply. This was not unusual. Emily waved back as if to say, 'Noted!' and she did it with a smile on her face in case it was a joke, to show that she had got it and she was amused. Dr. Muriel was one of those people who could help to simplify an idea and provide an answer to a problem if one were needed – and if not, she could complicate everything needlessly. Emily wasn't in the mood for complications or cryptic remarks. She went on her way.

But Dr. Muriel swooped across the road – a big, grey owl, Emily her helpless quarry. Why was everyone so friendly? You didn't move to London to have a chat. You moved to London to get on in life and get invited to sophisticated parties – not that Emily had had much success with either, to date.

'Terrible business!' said Dr. Muriel to Emily.

'Yes,' said Emily, not quite sure what she was talking about.

'You're a bright girl. You'll find something that's right for you...' Dr. Muriel saw that Emily had abandoned any attempt to pretend she understood the topic of conversation. She said, 'Vicky told me you were out of work again.'

Emily said, 'You should see the job adverts these days – it's all about "passion" and "commitment" and "making a difference". I'd just like to find an employer that will pay me a decent wage for doing a competent job. I don't want to give up a piece of my soul.'

'You rail against potential employers who treat their trivial business as though it were important, and yet you treat your important business – your life, your future – as though it were trivial. You most certainly do not just want to do "a competent job", Emily Castles. You are an inquisitive, fair-minded, insightful young woman who is easily bored. It's true that employers are continually letting you go, but it's because you have let them go long before it ever comes to that. You could do worse than go and work for Vicky, m'dear. There are always interesting dynamics in a staffroom (I should know), and of course, there are all those pushy parents intent on polishing pebbles and producing diamonds in two lessons a week during term-times, for £20 a week. I think you'll find it stimulating. I hope so, anyway.'

Emily would have liked to confide in Dr. Muriel about the blackmail and Victoria's video. But she had only known this secret for less than a day, and she didn't think it would be to her credit to spill it to the very next person she saw after Victoria told her about it. Instead she said, 'So are you going to a wedding?'

'Gracious, no! Weddings are awfully depressing, aren't they? They do have a tendency to make one feel suicidal. No, indeed. This afternoon I shall be attending an event that always makes me feel positively murderous.' And Dr. Muriel smiled wickedly and went on her way.

Showstoppers was in a red and yellow brick Edwardian building not far from the street where Emily lived. It would be pleasant to walk to work, she acknowledged – and it would be strange to be walking to school after all these years, even if it was to a performing arts school. Emily enjoyed a pleasant little frisson of nostalgia as she thought back to the days when she walked to school as a child in her blazer and grey and blue school uniform. It had always seemed sunny. For a moment she wondered whether this was a kind of false memory – the rosiness of an adult reflecting on her childhood – and then she realised that she probably only remembered sunny days walking to school because she would have got a lift when it was raining.

Victoria came out to greet her when she arrived at Showstoppers, gripping Emily by the shoulders and giving her a kiss on one cheek. She was wearing jeans and a white T-shirt, with a hideous pewter-grey loose-knit shawl draped over her shoulders that made her look fragile and tragic, as though her husband had been lost at sea and she had grabbed just *anything* to wear to keep herself warm while she walked along the shoreline, waiting for news of him. 'Hello, Ems,' said Victoria. 'Listen, you won't tell anyone here that I killed a man?'

'No,' said Emily. 'I won't do that.'

The dance school had once been a local primary school, so it had several large, airy rooms with wooden floors and high ceilings, a performance space where assemblies had been held, and a suite of tiny toilets for small children, as well as standard-sized facilities. The offices were upstairs on the first floor. It had been a long time since Emily had been in a place like this. She had forgotten about the shiny thick linoleum on the stairs, the worn banisters, the scratched wooden floors in the classrooms. From downstairs there drifted the plangent sound of the piano being played by unknown hands, and over the music she heard the excited, almost-mocking sound of children's laughter, and she was struck again with memories, as though the school was full of ghosts whispering about P.E. lessons and colouring-in.

Victoria opened the door to the office. 'Let me introduce you girls to each other,' she said in her weary, posh voice. 'People say "girls" now, right? I've been "a woman" since I was eighteen, but that was in the eighties. I've lived so long, we've all become girls again. I would say it's like a fabulous rejuvenation cream – except it only recategorizes you, it doesn't remove your wrinkles.'

Emily smiled at the girl behind the desk and raised her eyebrows to signal that she was slightly baffled. Did Victoria always go on like this?

'I'm Seema,' said the girl behind the desk, ignoring Emily's eyebrows. The trousers Seema were wearing were as white as her teeth, and her smile was as big as her hair, which had been backcombed and sprayed until it stood an inch above her scalp. She was plump and pretty. 'I don't mind being called a girl. They can chuck me in my grave when I'm ninety and say "here lies the old girl" and I won't mind. But then I won't mind about anythink much, will I, if I'm dead? You feeling old today, Victoria?'

'I am a bit.'

'Thought so. You only mention the nineteen eighties when you're feeling old. Ready for your holiday after this? You can have a nice rest.'

'Emily's here to help out while I'm away.'

'Yeah? Me and Emily'll run the place smooth as ice cream and twice as sweet, Victoria.'

'You are a darling, Seema. What would I do without you? It's too, too stressful.'

'About time you got some fresh air on them frown lines. Forget about this place next week, it's in capable hands. You'll come back and you'll wonder why you don't leave everythink to us every day.'

Seema was a white-trousered steamroller, trundling over all of Victoria's anxieties – and some of her self-esteem – and crushing them all, cheerfully.

Victoria picked up a folder from Seema's desk. She held it as far away from her face as she could to read it.

'You want your glasses on, Victoria,' said Seema.

'Oh, I know. I'm too vain. I think I'd rather be fitted with extendable arms than wear my reading glasses. Is this the list of new clients? I'd like Emily to interview the parents, get a feel for how we do things.'

'You want Emily to do the induction? What's she gonna say if she don't know the place?'

'Not an induction exactly... asking questions: a screening process.'

'*They're* supposed to ask questions, and *we're* supposed to have the answers. That's how it works usually, innit?'

'Oh, Seema. You are so terribly efficient,' said Victoria. 'But I think we should introduce a screening process, don't you? Whittle out the undesirables.'

'Undie-what? That's not a word your accountant would understand, Victoria. The bills don't pay themselves.'

'Actually, I rather think they do, with these electronic systems and direct debit and whatnot.'

'So long as they pay termly in advance, they're desirable, ent they?' Seema took the folder from Victoria and read aloud from it. 'Dolly, Kayleigh, Maqsood, Robin, DeShawn. Four, five, six years old, these kids – what harm can they do?'

'It's not the children I wanted to screen, so much as the parents...'

'I don't want Emily turning away potential clients because she's unfamiliar with how to run an establishment like this. No offence, Emily.'

How many jobs had Emily started where she had soon enough discovered that there was some kind of polite feud going on, with undercurrents of tension about who was really in charge and how things should be run? Too many; most of them; all of them. The thing about being here – or anywhere – on a temporary contract was that, ultimately, *she didn't care*. She smiled at Seema: a genuine, warm smile. Seema was posturing. Emily wanted to let her know that she, Emily, wasn't a threat.

'No, of course,' Victoria said, more vague than contrite. She picked up her handbag and felt around in it before bringing out something that Emily recognised: the video. 'Can you put this somewhere safe for me? Lock it away?' Victoria said to Seema.

'Is it for the show?' Seema said. 'I'll have to get Dizzy to bring the video cart down. I don't know if we've even got the screen set up.'

113

'Crikey, no! It's just something that needs to be locked away, very carefully, out of sight. I don't want it in the house. I can't deal with it now. I'll worry about it when I get back from holiday.'

'Oh?' said Seema. She looked as though she were about to burst out of her trousers with curiosity.

'Dirty video, is it? Found Piers's porn stash?' The dreadlocked head of a smiling man who Emily hadn't even noticed emerged with regal sedateness from behind Seema's desk, where he had been working on a cluster of electrical plug sockets set into the floor in the office. He was in his forties, tiny strands of silver hair twisted in among the black, as though his locks were magnetic and had attracted a powdering of iron filings that had been spilled on the floor near where he had knelt to work. He held a screwdriver and wore very dark blue overalls that had a few daubs of paint on them. There was no doubt in Emily's mind that he was the school's handyman. In fact, he did a bit of everything – technician, electrician, carpenter, caretaker and occasional chauffeur. He was indispensable because of his willingness to turn his hand to anything, though he wasn't especially skilled at any of them.

'Nothing like that, Dizzy,' Victoria said. 'It's a video I made when I was a student, with my boyfriend at the time, David Devereux. I don't want anyone to see it.'

'Oh!' said Seema.

Dizzy said respectfully, 'An acting video? My mistake, Victoria. Hello, Emily.'

Victoria said, 'Dizzy, you're not trying to fix the electrics yourself, are you? You need someone qualified.'

'Mr. Barrymore's helping me,' said Dizzy.

'Barry's helping you?' Victoria put her hands palm-out in front of her and made a 'window-washing' movement, fingers spread wide, as if trying to wipe away Dizzy's words where they hung in the air between them both. 'You *are* joking? Please don't let him anywhere near it. He's more likely to sabotage it than fix it. You know he wants me out of this place. I noticed the infant toilets didn't get blocked up once when he was away for his fortnight in Menorca.' She turned to Emily and said, 'Mr. Barrymore, our *horrible* landlord, is trying to get me to give this place up so he can sell it to developers to be made into luxury flats.'

Emily said, 'Hello, Dizzy.'

Seema said, 'I'm studying for a City & Guilds in building maintenance. I'd take a look at the wiring myself but I'm too busy.'

'Of course you are,' Victoria said. 'Right! I need to go and get changed. I need to rehearse the teachers' skit with Graham, he's over-creaking his Tin Man in my *Wizard of Oz* tap-dancing routine. He doesn't even have to tap dance, just gyrate his hips a bit. Some of the children have already arrived, and the rest will be arriving any minute. We've got the patrons coming in to give prizes. They'll need to be briefed. We've got the new parents coming; they'll need to be interviewed. We've got the current parents coming; they'll need to be avoided, especially if their children aren't being awarded prizes.'

There was suddenly a very unpleasant smell in the room. 'Oh my goodness!' said Victoria. 'What's that? Don't tell me we've got a problem with the drains?'

A sweaty white man with a bald head edged into the room – apparently he had been standing in the doorway for a short while. The man was about fifty years old, and he was wearing an England football shirt, which was made of white synthetic material with three blue lions embroidered on the left breast. Emily didn't recognise him and, given his age and physical condition, was inclined to disbelieve he played for the team. She took a dislike to him: she didn't approve of snoops. 'I think it's Precious,' the man said. 'I've been feeding her extra sausages to get her to be good.'

'Barry,' Victoria said, 'what on *earth* is Precious doing here?'

'You said you needed a real dog to play Toto,' Seema said. 'Mr. Barrymore's was the only one available at short notice. It seemed the best thing to do.'

'No trouble at all,' said Mr. Barrymore. 'Specially as we're only next door.'

Victoria walked around the desk behind Seema, and Emily followed her to see an extraordinarily ugly bulldog lying on a blanket. The dog sighed.

'If you brought this malodorous animal onto the premises as your first step in an eviction plan, you're more cunning than I thought,' said Victoria, opening a window in the office.

Mr. Barrymore laughed appreciatively and for slightly too long, as though he had met his favourite TV comedienne by chance in the supermarket and she had said something funny about the vegetables in his shopping basket. He said, 'There's another place I want you to look at in Crystal Palace, Victoria. Very modern. Much better appointed than this. I don't need Precious to persuade you. Soon as you see it, you'll love it.'

Victoria said, 'I'm going to get changed. Emily, do you know Morgana Blakely, the romance novelist?'

'I've heard of her,' said Emily. 'Is she coming?'

'Yes. She's Piers' aunty, and she'll be giving a prize to one of the students. You'll know her when you see her. She'll be wearing something ridiculous. Probably a hat.' From downstairs there was the sound of someone on the piano playing "Somewhere Over the Rainbow". Victoria listened for a moment and then continued, 'You know Dr. Muriel? And Midori? Midori's a Japanese girl. Goes by the stage name of DJ Hana-bi?'

'Yes,' said Emily. 'They both live on our street. I didn't know they were friends of yours.'

'Friends and neighbours and awfully good role models. They'll be giving prizes, too. They'll be along in a bit, so can you just keep them out of mischief? I can hear Samuel giving us a very big hint on the piano. I need to find Graham and get started rehearsing. Seema, dear, you can take care of the parents, but *please* will you let Emily talk to David Devereux when he gets here.'

'David Devereux's coming? Fella was in that spy thing? Black geezer? I thought he was in Hollywood.' Mr. Barrymore seemed impressed.

'Yes. So if you would be a love and get the electrics working? I don't know what's wrong with the wiring. I don't want the music cutting out when the tinies are doing their Flight of the Bumblebee. Graham and I can improvise, but the little ones can't – nor can the teenagers, come to that – and I don't want them being upset.'

Seema said, 'I need to talk to you, Victoria. There's a letter arrived here for you. It's a bit of a strange one. It's a personal letter, but I didn't realise. I'm afraid I opened it.'

'Oh, not now, Seema,' Victoria said. 'I really can't be doing with it.'

Victoria left. Mr. Barrymore left. Dizzy left. Seema said, 'Emily, have you seen that video? I need to lock it away somewhere. It was here on the desk.'

From downstairs came the sound of Victoria shouting, "Emileeeeeeee, Emileeeeeee. Can you come down? Morgana's here.'

Emily said to Seema, 'It can't have gone far. Can it?'

When Emily went downstairs to meet the famous romance novelist, Morgana Blakely, she immediately recognised her, just as Victoria had said she would. Morgana was indeed wearing a hat. It was a miniature top hat perched on the side of her head and held in place with hat pins and with a short veil attached to it, fashioned out of wire mesh. Emily had been to parties (or rather, she had waitressed at them) where canapés were served in the form of miniature fish and chips, or miniature burgers roughly the size of the circle made by joining the thumb and forefinger of one hand. Morgana's top hat was a bit like this. It had all the attributes of a normal top hat, but it was considerably smaller. If Morgana wasn't so imposing and hadn't just arrived to give prizes at her nephew's wife's stage school, Emily would have assumed she was in fancy dress.

Morgana must have been in her sixties – at least – but she had the youthful-looking skin of a woman who moisturises every day. She wore a purple trouser suit with a long purple velvet coat over it, trimmed in mauve marabou stork feathers, and she had applied flattering make-up: pale pink lipstick, black mascara, a touch of mauve eye shadow and a dusting of pink blusher. Her short, stylish hair was the colour of rich beef gravy.

Before Emily had to worry what to do with her, Dr. Muriel arrived. She and Morgana greeted each other like old friends, which is to say, they held hands, looked into each other's eyes and laughed.

Victoria came up to them. She was now wearing a blue pinafore dress and sparkly red tap shoes. She had put her hair in two long plaits, and she was still working at the strands of the left one as she walked.

'Something terrible has happened,' she said. 'I think we should call the whole thing off.'

'You always say that,' said Morgana. 'Things come together in the end, don't they?'

'No, it's worse than under-rehearsed dancers and disgruntled parents. I think we might be in danger. There's this video I made when I was a student...'

'Oh, Victoria!' said Morgana.

'Not that kind of video.'

'Who knows about it?' asked Dr. Muriel.

'I haven't told anyone,' Victoria said. 'Not a living soul.'

Emily checked her pulse. Yes, still alive.

Victoria said, 'It was a video I made with David Devereux when we were at drama school. He's been sending me poison pen letters.'

'Has he, indeed?' said Dr. Muriel.

'Bad things happen to people who watch that video.'

'How interesting,' said Dr. Muriel. 'Have you ever heard of a self-fulfilling prophesy?'

Morgana said, 'Tell us what happened, Victoria, in the order it happened.'

'I made the video with David. Twenty years ago a man died of a heart attack from laughing so much while he was watching it. David and I broke up even though we loved each other. The video turned up at the house a few weeks ago. David tried to enrol his daughter in the school a few weeks later. And then I started getting the letters.'

'You think David's still in love with you? He's invented a daughter and come back to claim you, and sending those letters is his way of doing it?' Morgana asked.

'We don't know for sure that David Devereux sent those letters,' said Emily.

A man whose face had been covered in silver face paint came up to Victoria. His limbs were encased in silver-sprayed cardboard, and he was wearing a small silver triangular hat. His costume was a boiler suit and a pair of Wellington boots. These had also been sprayed with silver paint. He said to Victoria, 'Midori just phoned. She's ill. She can't make it.'

'You see?' wailed Victoria. 'More bad luck!'

'I don't think it's anything to do with the video,' said the Tin Man. 'She's at home. She can't have seen it. Tummy trouble, she said.' And then, to Emily, 'Hello. I'm Graham.'

'Graham knows about the video?' asked Emily.

'Yes,' said Victoria. 'I had to tell him I'd brought it into the school. I think if you don't tell employees about this sort of thing – potential hazards in the workplace – you can get in trouble. Health and Safety.'

'I doubt the video *is* dangerous, Victoria,' said Dr. Muriel. 'Would it help dispel the myth if we were to watch it?'

'The video has disappeared,' said Victoria. 'It's out in the wild, so to speak, and now anyone could just pick it up and watch it, unawares.'

'Anyone with a VHS video player,' said Emily.

'Precious has disappeared,' Victoria continued. 'Dizzy has disappeared. Mr. Barrymore is still here. I wish he would disappear – I'd make him disappear myself if I could, though not until after he has fixed my electrics. As for Dizzy, he's what you might call a "bodger", but he does get things done in the end, and I do need to find him.'

'Seema said she might be able to fix the wiring,' said Emily. 'Shall I find her and ask her to do it?'

'I wish I could leave everything to Seema. Isn't she marvellous? But she's doing the induction with the parents. Emily, do you think you could have a look for Precious? You like dogs – can you see if you can coax her out? She's an evil-looking bulldog with a very low undercarriage. She stinks. Her name's Precious. Have you got a sausage or something to tempt her with when you find her?'

Emily did not. She thought she might not go and look for Precious. She said, 'I already met the dog, remember?'

'Oh, yes. I'm so stressed. I'm getting confused about things. Thank goodness you're here, Ems.'

Morgana said, 'What a shame I don't write mysteries, I could be noting all this down. It only really gets interesting for me when the love interest crops up. Can you do anything about that, Victoria?'

Just then, as if waiting for his cue – he was an actor, after all – the most handsome man Emily had ever seen walked through the door, accompanied by a small, beautiful, caramel-coloured child. It was David Devereux and Dolly. Dolly had long, curly hair that sprang out from her head as though someone had opened it to try to understand the workings and hadn't been able to fit everything back in again. David had eyes, hands, lips, teeth, a smile, a chest, a waist, long legs and strong arms – just like any other man, really. But the way they had all been put together seemed so much more appealing.

'Oh, Muriel,' said Morgana Blakely. 'Here's your answer, if you ever ask yourself why we agree to do these things – you've got your self-fulfilling prophesy video conundrum. And I've got this.'

'Hello, Victoria,' said David. They greeted each other like former lovers who still cared about each other, which is to say, they held hands and looked into each other's eyes, strange, tender expressions on their faces, as though they weren't sure whether they ought to say sorry about something.

'Emily,' Victoria said eventually, 'this is David. Would you mind looking after him? And Dolly, do you want to come with me and find some of the other children? One of the teachers will show you around. You can see how you like the place.'

'Victoria!' called David before she had gone too far. 'Did you ever have children?'

Victoria turned, Dolly's hand in hers. 'Yes,' she said. 'Three sons.'

She turned, and they walked away. Sunlight streamed from the tall windows along the corridor and dripped coppery highlights into Victoria's plaits and Dolly's liquorice-coloured curly hair: a woman dressed as a child from a story about a tornado-induced dream holding onto the hand of a child who was so beautiful Emily thought she looked as though she'd be able to create tornadoes and stories of her own one day.

'Emily!' whispered Dr. Muriel, interrupting Emily's reverie. 'I wanted to ask you about these letters Victoria's been receiving. We can't do it now. Shall we try to find a moment?'

'Seema could probably show you one,' Emily said. 'They've been coming to Victoria's house, but apparently one arrived at the school this morning.'

'Indeed? That's most interesting.' She turned to Morgana and indicated that they should head upstairs to the office. 'Shall we?'

'Must we?' said Morgana. She gave a little wave to Emily and David, and she took Dr. Muriel's arm as they walked up the stairs.

'Nice place,' said David to Emily. 'How long have you been working here?'

'About an hour.'

David laughed as though it was the cleverest thing anyone had ever said to him. Somewhere in the background, as more and more students arrived to take part in the show, Emily heard the sound of children's joyful voices, as though they had heard David laughing and wanted to join in. Emily was surrounded by an orchestra of happy sounds. It was all a bit disconcerting, but there was one thing she was sure of: it wasn't David who had sent those poison pen letters.

'Can I do anything useful?' asked David. It seemed a rhetorical question – what couldn't he do, with that smile? But Emily rallied and said, 'A dog's gone missing. You could help me find her.'

'I don't know much about dogs.'

Emily thought of her dog Jessie, her lovely old Golden Retriever who had died. She still missed Jessie and had thought her heart would break when she watched Jessie slip away, enfeebled by illness at the end. She said, 'Sometimes I think I know too much.'

'Come on, then! We'll make a great team. You don't mind if I keep my mobile on? I'm expecting a call from LA. They're probably not up and about this time of the morning. But you never know: the city that never sleeps.'

'Isn't that New York?'

David laughed again. 'There you go. Another thing you know more about than I do. We'll make a great team.'

Seema came bustling by, white trousers gleaming, floral top flowing. She was carrying a packet of dog biscuits and Dizzy's screwdriver. 'David!' she said. 'What an honour to meet you. I loved your work in *Spies Like Us*'. She smiled. She looked vivacious. Emily felt unaccountably jealous. Seema said, 'Emily, do you want a Bonio?'

Emily said, 'I'm trying to give them up.'

David laughed (again) and took the packet of dog biscuits. 'Good thinking. Seema, is it? Did I talk to you on the phone about enrolling Dolly? Don't worry, we'll find your dog.'

'It isn't my dog!' said Seema, horrified, as though he'd said 'Don't worry, we'll find your Nazi memorabilia.' Emily didn't much trust people who didn't like dogs. People who didn't know much about dogs were OK, of course. But there's nothing admirable about someone who tips over into active dislike. 'Our handyman's gone missing,' Seema continued. 'Black dude, blue overalls, dreads. If you see him...?'

David put his hand, almost, on Emily's waist as he escorted her out of the room. 'Don't worry,' he said to Seema. 'If we see him, we'll send him your way.'

'I'm doing the induction for the new parents,' Seema said. 'Most of them are here now. I do hope you'll join us, David.'

'Yeah, I will. Not sure if this place is quite right for Dolly, yet.'

Seema gasped in anguish and put one hand to her face as though he had slapped her.

'Kidding!' he said. 'I'm kidding, Seema. It's a great place. Any questions, though, I might as well ask Emily.'

Seema gave Emily a look of general disdain – so it was impossible to know whether she disapproved of Emily spending time with David or whether she simply felt that Emily couldn't be trusted to answer any questions about the school correctly (in which assessment she was, after all, perfectly correct). Then she bustled off again.

'I need to talk to Dr. Muriel before we go looking for Precious,' Emily said to David, leading the way up the stairs to the office. 'She and Morgana have been looking at a weird letter that arrived here for Victoria this morning.'

David didn't react – at least, he didn't react the way someone would react if they were responsible for sending the letter. He said, 'Is there anything about this place that isn't a little bit weird?'

When they got to the office, they saw that Dr. Muriel and Morgana had made themselves comfortable. They were drinking tea and chatting earnestly. There was a very large oval dish of sandwiches on the desk beside them, its cling film cover partially pulled back and several of the sandwiches missing.

'Where is Seema?' asked Dr. Muriel. 'The sandwich shop just delivered these. I think we need to fend for ourselves rather than get faint with hunger. Emily, you've been here all day, haven't you? I know it's barely midday, but if you don't eat now, it will be four o'clock before the show's over.

You'll be hungry if you don't eat a couple of sandwiches now.'

'I think we need to do something to help Victoria,' Dr. Muriel said. 'Poor woman is in meltdown.'

'I wish Piers were here,' said Morgana. 'But he's so often working on weekends.'

'Is Piers her husband?' asked David. 'Matinees are a killer. Is he in a show in town?'

'He's not an actor. I'm not quite sure what he does exactly. He's in the civil service.'

'Is he?' David looked interested. 'Is that a euphemism? I met a few ex-MI6 for that TV series I was in. Their families would have said something similar.'

Morgana paused before answering. She could have been pausing for effect, counting in her head, *one morgana blakely, two morgana blakely, three morgana blakely* before responding. Or there might have been something in what David said. 'Darling,' Morgana said eventually, 'I simply have no idea what Piers does. It's worthy but boring. Not the stuff of romantic heroes – or action heroes – I'm afraid.'

'Talking of action heroes,' David said, 'I hear the handyman's missing. I'll go and look for him. Where would he be?'

'Let me think,' said Morgana, 'I've been here often enough... Yes! He's got a shed round the back of the playground where he keeps his tools, next to the landlord's place. You could try there.'

David went off in search of Dizzy.

Morgana said, 'I think I'll go and see if Victoria needs help pacifying the non-prizewinning parents. I'll offer to send off a few signed books, that usually helps. If things get really fractious, I might have to agree to judge an under-sixteens flash fiction writing competition or something. Remember that time, a few years ago, Muriel, when we thought we'd have to get up and sing a song to calm everyone down?'

'I'm not sure it would have had a calming effect,' said Dr. Muriel. 'Everything seems much more under control here today. I doubt we'll feel called upon to participate in the performance.'

'You will come and join me soon, won't you?' said Morgana. 'The show will be starting any minute. Don't let me take my place on that stage all alone. Some of the numbers would seem interminably long if they weren't punctuated by your derisive snorting, cheering things along.'

When Morgana had gone, Dr. Muriel got up and closed the door. She said, 'I had a look at that letter. Curious, don't you think?'

'What does it say?

Dr. Muriel took a note that had been written in blue biro on blue stationery from her pocket and showed it to Emily before putting it back in her pocket again.

THE SHOW MUST GO ON
OR MUST IT NOT?
STOP IT, VICKY
OR BE STOPPED

'It seems to be a threat to disrupt the show, but it doesn't make much sense,' Emily said. 'There's no consistency or clarity about what they want her to do, even if she were inclined to follow their directions. It's as if sending the notes is more important than the threats they contain. The first note seemed to be a threat to tell Piers, then to tell everyone, then to tell people at the school. Maybe the sender just wants to frighten her rather than get her to do anything. It seems to be a bluff, doesn't it? I mean, we've all got secrets.'

'Interesting! And very perceptive. Here's another curious thing: Why would someone send a letter here all of a sudden when they had been sending them to her house?'

'Victoria thinks David sent them.'

'Do you?'

'No. But she thinks it's connected to the video, and no one knew about it except her and David and a few of the other students – and their tutor who watched it, who died.'

'That's what she says. But she really is a most indiscreet person. We'd be hard-pressed to find someone in this building who didn't know about the video. You and I and Morgana know. And Seema and Graham.'

'And Dizzy – and Mr. Barrymore. I think he was listening at the door when she mentioned it. But most of them only heard about it today.'

'Indeed. The question is, who knew *before* those letters started arriving. And why send them in the first place? If it was David, what would he hope to achieve? We need to take a look at that video, Emily.'

'It's gone missing. And so has Dizzy.'

'Well, David is looking for Dizzy, so let's you and I hunt the video together. Where should we look?'

'There's a cupboard somewhere with a video cart with a TV and video player on it. Seema mentioned it. We could try there. I'm not quite sure where it is...'

'Perfect! Can't be hard to find.'

Dr. Muriel opened the door to the office, and they set off. They tried the handles of the doors as they passed. Most opened onto classrooms. One opened onto a staffroom. One opened onto a small kitchen with a fridge, a kettle and a microwave. Eventually they found a door that looked promising. It was marked 'AV Cupboard', and it was locked or blocked from the inside. As Emily and Dr. Muriel pressed their weight against it, they heard the sound of David's mellifluous voice behind them. 'Maybe the door opens outwards, ladies. Have you tried it?'

He reached through their arms and tried it, but the door did not open outwards. It opened inwards like the others, and it was stuck. David laughed. He said, 'Sorry. I didn't mean to be a patronising git.'

'Any luck with finding Dizzy, David?' Dr. Muriel asked him. 'Did you see him?'

'Didn't see anyone except the landlord at the sink at his kitchen window – at least I suppose it was the landlord. Wearing an England shirt? Thuggish-looking bloke. But he gave me a big smile.'

'That sounds like a very practical and comfortable solution to the question of how best to avoid Victoria's end-of-term show,' said Dr. Muriel. 'Warm and cosy in his kitchen, out of sight and sound of a hundred-odd children, no doubt putting the kettle on. No wonder he was smiling.' She turned back to the door. 'Let's try this, then. On my count: one, two, three.'

The three of them pushed, and the door opened a little way and then opened further. It was blocked by a man's body lying on the floor. The man was wearing dark blue overalls. It was Dizzy.

David went over to him and put his fingers on Dizzy's neck to check if he was alive. Dizzy groaned, looked up, and said, 'Great admirer of your work, man.'

'You've been knocked unconscious,' said David. 'Looks like a blow to the back of your head.'

'Have I? Woah! How long have I been out? I was having this really nice dream.'

'Did you bring the video up here, Dizzy?' asked Dr. Muriel.

'I've got aspirations,' said Dizzy, sitting up and touching the back of his head delicately with his fingers. 'Acting – I'm drawn to the profession. That's why I work at this place. David Devereux: household name. Thought if I watched a vid from his early days, I might learn something.'

Emily stepped over him and pressed the narrow letterbox opening on the video player with her fingers. It flapped inwards, gently. She pressed the eject button anyway, just in case, but there was nothing in the machine. 'There's nothing here now,' she said.

'Perhaps we should get you to a hospital,' Dr. Muriel said to Dizzy. She leaned in to him and waggled her hand in his face. 'How many fingers am I holding up?'

'Three. No, two. No, three.'

'Sounds OK to me,' said Dr. Muriel. 'Of course, I'm not a medical doctor.'

'Someone knocked you on the head and stole the video?' asked Emily.

'Could be,' said Dizzy. 'Could be. They might of misunderstood the nature of the content of it. There's some unsavoury people about.'

'You didn't see who it was?' Emily asked.

'I didn't, Emily. Must of been a fella, though. Gave me a pretty good whack.'

Emily turned to David. 'You didn't see anything suspicious?' she asked. *When you were wandering around unaccompanied, supposedly looking for the man we've just found unconscious?*

'What's going on?' It was Victoria's voice behind them. She was now dressed in a smart black trouser suit, ready to host the afternoon's event. Emily was relieved to see that she was not wearing the shawl.

'Don't worry, Victoria,' said Emily. 'He's not dead.'

Victoria said, 'Everyone's downstairs ready to watch the show – everyone except you, Dr. Muriel – and I can't find that wretched dog.

Fortunately Graham and I can improvise. I think I have an "invisible dog" lead in the cupboard in the office. Who's not dead?'

'I'm not,' called Dizzy.

Victoria headed for the office, and they all went along with her – perhaps everyone was as curious as Emily to see what an 'invisible dog lead' might be. When they got there, they saw Seema and a police officer. Seema looked as though she had been crying.

'I told him you've got a show to put on,' Seema said to Victoria. 'I asked if he could wait to question you till afterwards, and he said yes.'

'Question me? What on earth about? *Is* someone dead?'

'No!' called Dizzy from the back of the group.

'Yes,' said the police officer. He was quite young, and he looked like a fitness instructor, which was a job he did in his spare time. 'Mr. Barrymore, your landlord. They found him at his place.'

'How long ago did he die?' asked Emily.

'I'm afraid I can't divulge. They're going through all that now. It looks as though he's been dead for some hours.'

'Was he watching a video?' asked Victoria.

'I can't say, madam.'

'Just tell me this.' Victoria's voice was slightly unsteady. She put her hands one on top of the other and placed them just under her clavicle as she drew a deep breath. She said, 'Was he smiling when he died? Would you say he had a rictus grin on his face?'

'I wouldn't say something like that, madam. That's not the sort of terminology we use in the reports.'

'Was anyone with him?' asked Emily.

'Only a dog. A bulldog. I'm afraid the animal is also deceased.'

'Who would kill a dog?' asked Emily. Now she was upset.

The policeman looked sympathetic. He turned towards Emily and put his hand out as though he was considering touching her arm to comfort her. But he didn't approach her. 'The dog wasn't killed, miss. It looked like natural causes.'

'Of course it did,' said Victoria. 'Of course it did.' She shook her head back and forth several times.

Seema said, 'The show's about to start. What do you want to do, Victoria? You want to call it off?'

'I'll go down,' said Victoria, 'and we'll carry on as if nothing had happened. If the children only learn from me that we have to carry on *no matter what happens in our personal lives*, they'll have learned the most important lesson about this profession... Officer, it's very kind of you to be so understanding. I'll talk to you when the show's over. Say about half past five? Dizzy? If you're well enough, I'll need you to operate the sound and lights, please.'

Victoria left the office, followed by Dizzy.

The policeman said, 'Does that lady think this is a murder enquiry?'

Seema said, 'I didn't do anything. I'm not responsible for what happened.' She looked as though she might cry again. She also left the office.

David said, 'I'd better go and find Dolly.' He took his mobile phone out of his pocket and looked at it, then put it back again. 'I'll keep this on silent.'

Emily, Dr. Muriel and the policeman were left in the office. The policeman said, 'Didn't I see you two at that bonfire party in the big house down the end of Trinity Road?'

'Wasn't that fun!' said Dr. Muriel, standing and making shovelling motions with her hands so he would see himself out.

Just before he closed the door to the office, the policeman said, 'The video that might hypothetically be in the video player of the house of the gentleman who died. What sort of video was it, do you think?'

'It was a video Victoria made when she was a student at drama school,' said Emily.

'Ah!' he said. 'I see.'

'Not that kind of video,' Emily said, closing the door.

When he had gone, she asked Dr. Muriel, 'If you really liked someone but you thought they might have done something stupid, should you speak up about it even though they might get in trouble?'

'Aha!' said Dr. Muriel. 'Now, we'll be addressing all sorts of questions like this at the next conference in Eastbourne. Or is it Torquay? Anyhow, it would be wonderful to have you come along and listen to some of the finest minds in Europe debate such conundrums, both trivial and meaningful. It gets very heated. Most amusing. There is no right or wrong, of course. Only brilliant arguments from all sides.'

'What I'm trying to say,' said Emily, 'is do you think David could have bashed Dizzy on the head? He was gone for ages before he suddenly "found" him with us.'

'He doesn't strike me as a basher. And what's his motivation? No, it doesn't follow.'

'But then he said he waved and smiled at Mr. Barrymore in his kitchen window. But the policeman said that Mr. Barrymore had been dead for some time.'

'Indeed, indeed – most suspicious. But, although that young policeman wasn't prepared to say anything, I do think Mr. Barrymore might have been watching Vicky's video, don't you?'

'Yes.'

'So it follows that if Mr. Barrymore stole that video, then it was probably Mr. B who bashed Dizzy.'

'Yes. But you don't think the *video* killed Mr. Barrymore, surely?'

'No, I don't... Good Lord!'

'What?'

'What's that frightful noise?'

Emily had also heard the noise coming from downstairs. It was a sawing sound. Last-minute repairs? Perhaps Dizzy's head injury had been more serious than anyone realised and he was running amok with power tools. She listened carefully. 'I think it might be the Flight of the Bumblebee.'

'Good. Good. First song of the afternoon. It means we've got a long, long time till the prize-giving. Morgana will never forgive me if I don't sit through the show and watch it with her, but I've put up with worse things than Morgana's unforgiveness. Come on. We need to do a little sleuthing for ourselves. We know what we do not have: we do not have a video that is such bad luck or so horrendous to watch that it kills people, because that would be daft. We do not have an actor who is a murderer. We do have an injured man, a dead man and a dead dog.'

'And we have poison pen letters,' said Emily. 'I have a theory about who might have sent those.'

'Do you? Marvellous! Then we'll do some confronting later on.'

'Not on stage? Not in front of the children?'

'No, my dear. That would be a denouncement. That wouldn't do at all. A denouncement is public and upsetting. A confrontation is by invitation only and most satisfying. We'll do the confronting shortly before the policeman comes back, perhaps. When all the parents and the children are gone.'

'What if that policeman wasn't a real policeman? What if he was an actor who'd been hired to pretend that Mr. Barrymore was dead, to frighten Victoria?'

'He was rather young and handsome, wasn't he? He recognised us, though, didn't he? And he seemed rather sweet on you. He kept smiling and looking at your arm. No, I'm afraid there's nothing else for it. We have to go and confront the thing we fear most.'

'Victoria's video?'

'Only indirectly. No, I meant death.'

Emily and Dr. Muriel went back down the stairs, meaning to reach Mr. Barrymore's home by cutting across the playground. Before they got to the door that led outside, they passed the assembly hall and peeked in through a small window set into the door at about head height. Around two dozen small children were on stage, dressed in black and yellow striped costumes. Dizzy was at the technician's desk, operating the spotlights, sound effects and backing tapes.

The parents and siblings of the students were a warm and appreciative audience. At the front, positioned to half-face the stage, half-face the audience – like the Queen at a command performance of the Royal Variety Show – Morgana sat alone between an empty chair that had been meant for Midori, the Japanese DJ with the delicate constitution who had cancelled due to illness, and an empty chair that was meant for Dr. Muriel, the hearty British professor who would rather face death than sit through a musical theatre show by Victoria's students.

They started to creep away from the assembly hall towards the door to the playground but hadn't gone more than two or three steps before Victoria came up behind them and stopped them. She was back in her blue pinafore, though this time she was wearing red Wellington boots rather than sparkly shoes. 'Funnier, don't you think? And anyway I'm not going to do the tap routine.

Graham's an incompetent hoofer, though I can hardly blame him. It's my fault for leaving it so late to rehearse.'

Victoria's hair was braided into two plaits again. She had an 'invisible dog' lead in her right hand – a stiff piece of red leather that reached almost to her ankles when she held the top loop of it at waist height, with a circle of red leather at the bottom, facing forward, as though strained by the neck of a smallish, eager dog that Emily and Dr. Muriel could not see.

'I'm going to go to the police after the show and confess everything,' Victoria said. 'That video has done enough damage. I've got blood on my hands. Piers will be relieved, at least. He thinks I spend too much time at Showstoppers and not enough time at home.'

'Where is Piers?' asked Dr. Muriel. 'I'd have thought he'd be here to support you.'

'I know,' said Victoria with cool irony. 'What sort of man puts Queen and country before his wife's end-of-term show at her drama school?'

'The sort of man who doesn't want his wife to have a nervous breakdown,' said Dr. Muriel.

Victoria put her right hand to her eyebrows and leaned forward and swivelled a half turn on her right heel as though she planned to dance the hornpipe. But she was only manoeuvring to look through the window in the door to the assembly hall. 'Ugh,' she said. 'Did you notice that? The lights keep dipping, and there's something not right with the sound levels. If Mr. Barrymore weren't dead, I'd kill him myself.'

'I suppose you won't have to move the school now that he's dead?' said Emily.

Victoria twisted her mouth, as if she was slightly ashamed of herself for what she had just said. 'Yes. I hadn't thought about that... Poor old Barry. The electrics are playing up, and he's not even here, so I feel a bit guilty that I ever implied he could be responsible. Though I do have my suspicions that the infant toilets won't be blocking up again in future... Where *are* you two going? Don't let the kids see you if you're nipping outside for a smoke. And please, please, please make sure you come back for at least part of the show. The finale's going to be great. I've had a brainwave and changed *everything* at the last minute.'

'We won't miss your teachers' skit,' said Dr. Muriel. 'What a shame you won't be tap dancing. That's always my favourite part.'

'Don't you worry, we're all coming on at the end – teachers, tinies, teenagers – and we're doing a group tap dance then. Samuel has briefed them, and they adore him and listen to what he says, so I hope it won't be too chaotic. Graham and I will just be singing for our skit, and I'll do a bit of business with the dog lead, and maybe a cartwheel, and hope these boots don't fall off. Graham has a wonderful voice, but the less he moves on stage this afternoon, the better, or we won't have anyone sign up for dance class and choreography next term and Seema will have my guts for garters.'

'Where is Seema?' asked Emily.

'She's taken the screwdriver, and she's gone to have a look at the fuse box under the stage, even though I've begged her to leave it alone. She's very tight-fisted with the accounts, so maybe she feels responsible for being a cheapskate and not getting a qualified electrician in, and she's trying to make amends. Although, doing it by killing herself is not the best way. Don't you think?'

'Well, if we see her, we'll intervene,' said Dr. Muriel. 'We don't want another dead body or a serious injury.'

'Oh, I don't think there's any question of that now that the video is at Barry's house under police guard. I do feel a tremendous amount of relief, actually. So long as it's evidence, they'll have to keep it under lock and key. And after that I'll just ask them to destroy it for me. I'm sure they'll be glad to help as I'm going to cooperate fully – it should keep the paperwork down.'

'You're not seriously going to confess to murder?' asked Emily.

'Living in a house with one man and three teenage boys, I sometimes think that going to prison is the only way I could get any peace,' said Victoria. 'But no, I'm not going to confess to killing anyone. Piers is right. Dr. Muriel's right. A video can't really be bad luck, no matter that David and I used to joke about it after our poor tutor died. But ever since that video turned up at the house, there's been trouble. I wonder if someone's heard me talk about the history of it and they're trying to frame me – I can't think *who* because I hardly breathed a word to anybody.'

'Indeed,' said Dr. Muriel. 'Interesting theory. Here's another for you: might someone be trying to attach some scandal to the name of David Devereux?'

'Could be.'

'Do you still think David sent you those letters?' asked Emily.

'I rather liked Morgana's theory that perhaps he was sending them because he wanted to get my attention, maybe even as a way of getting back together with me. But earlier on today, when I held his hand for the first time after all those years, there was no spark. And Dolly's no pathetic invention to give him an excuse to visit the school – she really is his daughter. She looks just like him.'

'Still, someone sent the letters,' said Emily.

'And whoever it was threatened to stop the show in the latest note,' said Dr. Muriel.

'Did they, indeed? I shan't say "over my dead body!"' said Victoria with a wink. The music coming from the assembly hall changed to jolly, comedic piano music, played very fast. 'Oof!' Victoria said. 'Good old Samuel! That number's the one before mine and Graham's – I'd better go.' She adjusted the invisible dog lead, pretending the unseen animal was tugging at the collar. With a backward flick of her head and a jaunty kick of her right foot, she dashed off after it in time to the music, towards the classroom nearest the assembly hall that was serving as a dressing room for the show.

Emily and Dr. Muriel went into the playground. The hopscotch-covered tarmac of the primary school days was now converted into a pleasant courtyard seating area, with wooden benches and raised flower-beds, and shady areas provided by wooden arches covered in vines and clematis, the landscaping reminiscent of holidays Victoria and Piers had enjoyed in Provence.

They could see the shed at the far end of it, where Dizzy kept his tools. Next to it, within the walled perimeter of the grounds, abutting the school building, was the caretaker's cottage that had been the home of the landlord, Mr. Barrymore. A thin blue and white strip of police tape ran between the front of the cottage and the playground.

Dr. Muriel put her hands in her pockets and strolled next to Emily in a hopelessly suspicious-looking way, as though she were a prisoner of war in a German camp, planning to distribute sand dug from an escape tunnel onto the ground as they walked. Emily was worried that at any minute her companion might actually start whistling.

'I've got a bad feeling about all this,' Emily said. 'The poison pen letters were meant to frighten Victoria, but now that the video's no longer in her possession, the notes no longer have any effect. I think Victoria might be in danger.'

'Do you know, m'dear, I agree with you.'

'Should we go and stand guard by the stage, in case we need to do something? Or should we call the police?'

'Knowledge is what we need: "intel". If we don't know what we're looking for, we won't know how to stop it. I don't suppose we can get inside the house here, but there's nothing to stop us peering through the window. First things first: the shed.'

The door to the shed was padlocked and didn't open when they pulled at it. They stood side by side at the two small square windows on it and looked into the darkness inside. But nothing looked out of place or suspicious. They turned and stood with their backs to the shed and looked over to Mr.

Barrymore's home, to their right. It was also in darkness. The kitchen window faced them. It appeared to be positioned above a sink, where Mr. Barrymore might very well have stood and smiled at David Devereux while he was doing the dishes or filling the kettle for a cup of tea – if only he hadn't already been dead.

'The policeman didn't say where they found him,' said Emily. 'If someone wanted to frame Victoria for murder, or make David look like a liar, could they have propped Mr. Barrymore's body up there, at the sink?'

'Interesting,' said Dr. Muriel. 'It makes a liar of David, certainly. But it doesn't put Victoria at the scene.'

Dr. Muriel pressed the end of her stick into the blue and white tape, moving it close enough to the cottage so that she and Emily could press their faces up against the glass of the living room window. They could see the young policeman inside in the gloom. 'You know,' said Emily, 'if someone wanted to harm Victoria or at least humiliate her and stop the show, wouldn't they choose her *Wizard of Oz* number to do it?'

'We're running out of time, then, m'dear. We urgently need to get ourselves a clue.'

The policeman came to the door of the house and opened it. He looked at Emily, and his hand floated up towards her elbow, tenderly. He didn't quite touch her, and he let his hand drop again as he said, 'Don't worry about the dog, miss. I don't think it suffered at all.'

Emily said, 'You can call me Emily.'

'James,' said the policeman.

'Constable James,' said Dr. Muriel, 'what are you doing lurking about in the gloom back there? Even at your young age, it can't be very good for your sight.'

'The fuse has gone. All the electricity's off.'

'Has it, has it, has it, is it?' said Dr. Muriel. 'Hmmmm. Dodgy wiring, perhaps? Tell me, was he found here in the kitchen, holding on to the taps?'

'You know I can't tell you that, madam.'

'Doctor.'

'Do you need one?' The policeman looked alarmed. His hand floated up, now, towards Dr. Muriel's elbow.'

'You may call me "doctor". But I don't insist on it. As you wish.'

'Oh, I see.' James looked at Emily and widened his eyes a bit to signal that he hoped she'd let on whether or not Dr. Muriel was teasing him. Emily grinned back.

'Were the taps metal?' said Dr. Muriel. 'Can you tell me that?'

'Well, I don't see what else they'd be made of,' said the policeman, a bit sulkily.

Dr. Muriel said, 'Here are the facts, as you have hinted at them or (in the case of the taps) confirmed them: Mr. Barrymore, a most unscrupulous landlord, a saver of pennies and cutter of corners, was found here at the sink, gripping the metal taps and staring out the window, with a ghastly grin on his face. The electricity was off, a fuse apparently having blown.' Dr. Muriel turned to Emily. 'What do you make of that, Emily?'

'The metal taps were live, somehow? He went to fill the kettle or wash his hands and he was electrocuted, and that caused a short circuit and blew a fuse?'

'Precisely!'

'Well, yes,' conceded James the policeman. 'It could be something like that.'

'The bulldog, Precious, was lying in the living room, teeth bared in the approximation of a human smile, having been electrocuted also because some part of her body was touching a lamp or some other electrical apparatus, which had also gone live.'

'She didn't suffer at all,' James said to Emily. 'I really think she didn't.'

'That's very clever,' said Emily to Dr. Muriel. 'Shouldn't you save it all for the confrontation?'

'That wasn't the confrontation, it was the denouement. And yes, I'll have to go through it all again. But let's consider it a dress rehearsal. It is a show business event, after all.'

'So it was natural causes?' Emily said. 'That means Victoria's not in danger. David Devereux's not a liar. We can go in and watch the show.'

'David Devereux?' said James. 'The actor in that spy thing? Isn't he supposed to be going to Hollywood?'

'Goodbye, Constable,' said Dr. Muriel. 'Come, Emily. If we hurry, we'll catch Victoria's performance. She's a talented actor, with wonderful comic timing. I won't say she's wasted here, but there's no match for her in any of the shows currently playing in the West End.'

They rushed back to the assembly hall, where they waited for the sound of applause to signal the end of the current number before Emily slipped in discreetly at the back of the audience, while Dr. Muriel went through a side door and took her place next to Morgana Blakely, whose face was so pinched with fury at being left alone that it looked as though her features were trying to shrink themselves to match the size of the tiny top hat she was wearing.

There was a space in a row at the back, three seats in next to David Devereux – the only space Emily could see, though she didn't look very hard. David saw her approaching, bent low as though she was a giantess who feared catching her hair in overhead pylons, and he moved up and moved Dolly up next to him, so Emily could take the seat on the end. He smiled and put his arm across the back of Dolly and reached to Emily's shoulder and gave it a squeeze, pressing his leg into Dolly's and Dolly's whole body into Emily, so for a moment they were all three of them scrunched up and cute-looking like a family of foxes in a den.

'Victoria'll be hilarious!' he whispered. 'If she's anything like she was at drama school. Wait till you see this.'

To the right, about halfway down the auditorium, Emily noticed a gleam of white as Seema edged her way in and stood quietly watching, back against the wall. White trousers really were distracting when worn by audience members, Emily thought. It was almost as bad as people eating popcorn in the cinema or texting on their mobile phones. Because of the trousers, she couldn't help tracking Seema's movements as she moved slowly to the back of the hall and then went to stand by Dizzy, where he operated the mixing desk for the sound and lights for the show.

Emily wasn't a regular theatre-goer, and she found she was summarising her reactions to the performance as though sending postcards to herself: *Victoria was very funny, and Graham was a little stiff in his movements but had an extraordinarily deep and attractive vibrato voice. Victoria's cartwheel was hilarious! 'Somewhere Over the Rainbow' was beautiful, and when she sang it, a capella, Victoria made almost everyone cry.*

Dolly held Emily's left hand in her right hand, and her father's right hand in her left as she sat between them. Emily wished that everyone she had ever known – everyone she had ever worked for or with in a temp contract in a miserable job – could be here to see their little group and speculate that Emily was somehow connected to David Devereux. She sent herself a little postcard about it: *On her way to Hollywood!*

David leaned over and whispered, 'She's great, isn't she? Remind me to tell you about this video we made when we were students. It was hilarious. You'll laugh your socks off.'

Remind me to tell you *when*? When we're on a date? When you come to pick me up from my next temp job in your Bentley or your Lamborghini? When we're flying to Hollywood together?

David bent and kissed Dolly's adorable head. He laughed as if Victoria's *Wizard of Oz* skit was the funniest thing he had ever seen and this was the happiest day of his life. His laughter carried, and a few people looked round to see what was going on and then smiled when they saw it was David Devereux, and he really was laughing at the show.

Behind them, Emily was aware that Seema was agitated, whispering to Dizzy about something. Perhaps she was disappointed that there was to be no tap dancing routine from Victoria? Or perhaps she was jealous that Emily was sitting next to the world's most good-natured handsome man.

In the classroom across the corridor that was serving as a dressing room, out of sight of the audience, all the members of Showstoppers were assembled, their small sweaty feet laced into their tap shoes, ready to take the stage for the final number, their small sweaty hands linked together as they prepared to come on in tightly-squished, snaking rows and then form one big circle together.

Victoria and Graham took their bow. Next to Emily, David whooped and blew three wolf whistles through his fingers. Victoria smiled and nodded her head once in his direction in acknowledgement, one professional to another, just like any other seasoned performer glad to see that one of their kind is 'in' to see the show.

'Brava!' shouted Dr. Muriel in her seat near the front, for all the world as if she were at the opera in Italy, where it's usual to match the gender of the exclamation to the person who is being praised.

'Brava!' If she had meant the praise for both Graham and Victoria, she would have shouted 'Bravi! Had her praise been meant just for Graham, she would have shouted 'Bravo!' Presumably she meant no offence to Graham by singling out Victoria – they were neighbours, after all. And Victoria was the school's artistic director and owner. Also, her cartwheel had been magnificent, as had her 'Somewhere Over the Rainbow'.

Victoria and Graham left the stage with a final wave to the audience, Victoria pretending to be led off by the invisible dog, to the amusement of Dolly and the other children in the audience, who shrieked in recognition of a kind of magic that needed them to 'see' it and believe in its charming illusion. Emily thought of her dog, Jessie, who had died and left a kind of invisible dog in her place which Emily 'saw' sometimes when she was tired or lonely, or when she simply forgot that Jessie had died. She wasn't too old to believe in magic, even if it made her feel sad sometimes.

The lights went down, and there was no music, only the swelling sound, stage left – to the right of the audience – of a hundred pairs of tap shoes beginning to beat a rhythm in the dressing room as the children prepared to come on. *It was very theatrical! So effective!* Emily postcarded to herself, enjoying the build-up. She began to think she should go to the theatre more often.

The children began to cross the corridor from the dressing room, heading towards the back of the stage where they would come on, though their performance had already begun. The sound of their tapping feet grew louder.

'Oh my God!' shrieked Seema white trousers gleaming where she now stood where she had first come in at the side of auditorium. 'Oh my God! Tap shoes! They're wearing tap shoes! All them sweaty little feet in metal and leather! Oh my God! Oh my God!'

Emily thought that if she were in charge of this place – which she was not because if the past was anything to go by, then for the rest of her life she was only ever going to have crappy administrative jobs, working for others, for a pitiful wage – she would send Seema on a management course to help her cope with change. Victoria had decided at the last minute to put the children in tap shoes for the final number. So what? So far, it sounded great.

But Dr. Muriel was on her feet at the front now, waving her walking stick in the air. 'Emily!' she shouted. Dr. Muriel was not the sort to try to storm the stage at a children's end-of-term show so she could join in the dancing – she had plenty of limelight during her day job, where she frequently addressed large conferences on her specialist subjects: ethics and philosophical conundrums. Even if Dr. Muriel did plan to storm the stage, there was no reason for her to call for Emily to join in. So it was something else...

Suddenly, Emily understood.

She jumped to her feet. She rushed to the technician's desk where Dizzy was standing and began pulling at wires and plugs, screaming, 'Turn it off! Turn it off!' If she could just expose two live wires and touch them together, she might stand a chance of tripping the fuse and killing the power – if she didn't kill herself first.

At the front, Dr. Muriel had whisked Morgana Blakely's miniature top hat from her head and now skimmed it onto the stage, where it skidded across the boards, sparking as the mesh veil attached to the hat and the hat pins that had secured it caught on a live wire or wires poking from beneath the stage, not far from the spot where Victoria had been performing her *Wizard of Oz* routine.

Morgana got to her feet and took action. 'No children on stage!' she commanded. 'Victoria, do you hear me? Graham! Don't let the children on the stage!'

Graham the Tin Man appeared through the side door in the assembly hall nearest to the stage, trying to make sense of what was going on. Dr. Muriel didn't hesitate. She grabbed his triangular hat and threw it towards the location of the exposed live wires on stage in front of her. She was a frequent guest lecturer on cruise ships and was an expert player of deck quoits (donut-shaped, heavyish objects made of rubber or rope, guaranteed not to bounce and go over the side), so her missile struck its target effectively. Sparks flew, and a hissing sound came from the stage.

In the background, the ominous thrumming of two hundred tap shoes continued, the children held at bay as Morgana had instructed, though it seemed Victoria was determined that, somehow or other, even if out of sight of the audience, the show would go on.

Dr. Muriel next threw her stick with its metal band around the tip (which didn't have any effect, though it made an impressive rattling sound), then she removed her jacket and threw it metal-button side down, causing more sparks and then, at last – whether through Dr. Muriel's interventions or Emily's – the fuses blew, the lights went off. Everyone was safe.

There was silence. Even the tap shoes had ceased tapping. There was darkness except for smears of late-afternoon sunlight coming through the cracks in the blackout curtains that had been hung at the tall windows along the left-hand side of the auditorium. Then there was spontaneous, rapturous applause from children and parents, and whoops and whistles, and then the sound of scraping chairs as the audience got to their feet in a standing ovation. At the periphery of her vision, Emily caught a flash of white as Seema turned and ran out through the door at the back of the assembly hall.

Dizzy had seen it, too. 'Oh no you don't, missy!' he called as he rushed out after her.

David Devereux had joined Emily near the technician's desk, where she stood with wires and plugs in her hands. He had Dolly with him – she didn't look frightened. She was young enough to think the finale might have been part of the show.

'Emily!' said David. 'Girl, that was brave of you.'

'*Now* we can have the denouement,' said Emily, shaking a bit – with shock, she thought, rather than electrical energy.

David reached over and grabbed her arm and pulled her towards him, and he kissed her.

So that's what you do when something I say isn't particularly funny, thought Emily. She resolved to be less amusing in front of handsome actors in future.

David's phone rang, and he answered it, 'Yes, yes... Yes! Yeah, I can. Yeah. OK, buddy,' while nodding and pretending to listen to Dolly, who was asking him a question.

'Daddy,' she said, 'is this my new school?'

'No, babe.' He finished his call. He put his hand on Dolly's head, smoothing her gorgeous curls, and he smiled at Emily.

'But I like it here, Daddy. I like Toto. I liked the ninja part at the end.'

David laughed his beautiful laugh, as if inviting the angels to join in. He said, 'Yeah, babe. It's great, isn't it? But I just got the call. We're moving to LA.'

***

A little later on, in Victoria's kitchen at her house opposite the flat where Emily lived, Dr. Muriel – jacket back on, stick propped against the desk – poured tea for Victoria, Emily and a hatless Morgana while they discussed the day's events. It was five o'clock, and they were all rather hungry, so Victoria split and toasted eight spicy fruit tea cakes, two at a time, in her expensive stainless steel toaster, and Emily stood next to her and buttered them and piled them onto a plate. Victoria was back in her jeans, white T-Shirt and pewter shawl, something like her fifth costume change of the day.

It had already been agreed that they had all been wonderful, and very brave, and they had praised each other accordingly. Now they were pondering the motives of the person who had nearly killed a hundred children on a Saturday afternoon in south London.

'Seema sent those poison pen letters?' asked Morgana.

'It was a bit of a giveaway when she produced another one this morning, saying it had been sent to Showstoppers instead of being sent to your house,' said Emily, taking her place at the table and picking up her cup of tea.

'As if I didn't have enough to worry about,' said Victoria, 'with the end-of-term show.'

'That was rather the point,' said Dr. Muriel. 'Seema thought the letters would tip you over the edge and you would stand down from running the school and let her take your place. She was very jealous of your success.'

'And like a lot of people who aren't very bright,' said Emily, 'she couldn't see why you were in charge and she wasn't. She liked following processes, and she found your creative management style irritating and threatening, especially your last-minute changes of plan. She thought that all she had to do was replace you, instead of learning the skills that would earn her the right to take over.'

'But I don't get it,' said Victoria, bringing the plate of tea cakes to the table and taking a seat next to Morgana. 'How did she know about the video?'

'You told her,' said Dr. Muriel, stretching for a tea cake. 'You told everyone.'

'Yes, but not until today.' Victoria nudged the plate in Dr. Muriel's direction so she could reach the food without embarrassing herself.

'You told me yesterday,' Emily said.

'You must have told Seema about the video a while ago,' said Dr. Muriel. 'I'd guess it was not long after your tutor's widow sent it to you out of the blue.'

'Poor Bill,' said Victoria, chomping on a buttery toasted tea cake. 'I don't remember saying anything to Seema. But she was a very good listener – she always seemed so sympathetic.'

'You didn't feel you could say anything to Piers,' said Morgana. 'Who else were you to turn to?'

'And you are terribly indiscreet,' said Dr. Muriel, offering the plate of tea cakes to Emily. 'I knew that Emily had lost her job, for example, only hours after Emily herself had told you.'

'Oh, Ems,' said Victoria. 'I know I offered you some work, but I think you might need to go back to the agency on Monday. I'm not sure we'll be up and running at Showstoppers for a while. You know?'

'That's OK, Victoria,' said Emily. 'I'm used to it. Thanks for asking me, anyway. You did tell Seema about that video. Then when David tried to enrol Dolly at Showstoppers, it gave Seema the idea of sending the poison pen letters and hinting that David was responsible, to upset you.'

'But what about Mr. Barrymore?' said Victoria. 'Yes, he was an ugly, bald fat man in an England shirt who tried to get me to give up my school premises so he could turn it into overpriced flats for young professionals – but that didn't mean he deserved to die.'

'He was the one who knocked Dizzy on the head,' said Emily. 'He'd been standing at the door to the office and overheard that there was a video you'd made with your boyfriend when you were a drama student. I think maybe he thought it would be, you know...'

'Stimulating, rather than artistic,' said Dr. Muriel, dabbing with a handkerchief at a spot of melted butter that had dripped onto her jersey.

'He certainly seemed very keen to get a look at it,' said Emily. 'I can't believe I thought David might have bashed Dizzy.'

'It's not such an outrageous idea,' said Dr. Muriel. 'After all, David Devereux does sometimes seem to be too good to be true.'

'Never mind him,' said Morgana. 'Wasn't there also a dog that died? Killing a dog is unforgiveable.'

'I think Seema was responsible for the death of both landlord and dog,' said Dr. Muriel. 'The police are interviewing her now, of course. But I think they'll discover her motive was to drive Victoria to have a nervous breakdown and hand over the daily running of the school to Seema, while also removing any worries about Showstoppers having to move to new premises, of course. It wasn't very far from the school to the landlord's cottage. Seema could have nipped down there at any time and tampered with the wiring – she seemed to fancy herself as something of dab hand electrician, on top of everything else.'

Emily continued, 'The "rictus smile" on Barrymore's and Precious's faces was caused by the electric shocks they received when Seema went to the cottage and tampered with the wiring earlier this morning. Seema would have seen Dizzy swipe the video from her desk and then seen Mr Barrymore sneaking off after him–'

Dr. Muriel interrupted excitedly, 'And she'd have known she had just enough time to go to the cottage and wire up the taps in the kitchen. The current passing through him would have made the landlord's body stiffen, his hands gripping the taps and keeping him standing upright. It would have contorted his face into something that David Devereux might have mistaken for a smile as he walked past the kitchen window.'

'Mr. Barrymore didn't die laughing,' said Emily, 'though when you asked James, the police constable, and he didn't deny it, Victoria, it fitted with your "dying of laughter" theory about the video. Of course, Seema knew it would.'

Dr. Muriel said to Victoria, 'But still you refused to give up on the show and stand down from the school. So next Seema tried tinkering with the wiring at the school so that when the metal of your tap shoe struck the live wires poking out from just under the stage, you'd get a shock. The faulty wiring would be blamed on Mr. Barrymore or Dizzy, or both.'

'Poor Dizzy!' said Morgana.

'Poor old Barrymore!' said Dr. Muriel.

'Poor Precious,' said Emily.

'I feel very ashamed that I didn't realise Dizzy had acting aspirations,' said Victoria. 'You know he's the one who chased down Seema and held onto her until the police arrived? He'd do anything for this place – he doesn't always do it very well, of course. But he does it with a true heart and a great deal of enthusiasm. I've put in a good word at our old drama school. He's auditioning for a summer school for mature students. David Devereux is going to coach him for his audition speech before he gets on the plane to Hollywood.'

'Why did David try to enrol his daughter at Showstoppers if he knew he might be going to LA?' asked Emily.

Victoria laughed, slightly bitterly. 'If every actor who had ever got the call from Hollywood – or been told they were down to the last two for a part in a movie or a starring role in the theatre – if every one of those actors just put their life on hold and waited to hear if it would happen, then they'd never get married; their children would never get an education; their bills would never get paid. You have to assume it will never happen and go about your business accordingly and get your car taxed and pay your TV licence and enrol your children for music lessons and stage school and state school. If it happens, as least you can cancel. If it doesn't, well... at least you're covered for the basics, and you can work towards the next audition and hope it will happen for you next time.'

'Victoria's still up for Desdemona in Branagh's *Othello*,' said Morgana.

'Technically,' said Victoria. 'Though that was nearly twenty years ago, and the film has been made and shown in cinemas and is now available on DVD. I think if they cast me in that part now I'd be inclined to sit up in bed and punch his lights out if Othello tried to stifle me.'

'Punch whose lights out?' asked Emily, impressed. 'Othello's or Kenneth Branagh's?'

'Emily and I have tried to piece together Seema's movements,' said Dr. Muriel, making an effort to get the conversation back to the events of that afternoon. 'The memory of a glimpse of her white trousers every now and then has worked like a very low-tech tracking device.' She chortled at the idea of it. 'She disappeared just before your *Wizard of Oz* number – we think she was under the stage with a screwdriver – and reappeared again to watch the results of her handiwork.'

'I wonder if Seema thought it would kill me,' said Victoria. 'Or if she just wanted to give me a shock.'

They heard the sound of the key in the lock, then Piers' voice calling out as he came through the door after a day at work. 'Victoria?'

They heard Piers hang up his coat, find a place for his laptop computer, wash his hands in the sink in the downstairs bathroom.

Morgana said to Victoria, 'With your last-minute change of plan, all those children in tap shoes with metal plates on the bottom for the finale, in a big snaky line, joined together with damp hands and sweaty feet...' She shuddered. 'What might have happened just doesn't bear thinking about.'

Victoria called out to her husband, 'In here, darling!'

'Thank God you're home,' he said as he walked into the kitchen. 'You won't believe the day I've had.'

REAL ELVES

'I want you to think of all the ways you could injure a child,' said Miranda. She was dressed as an elf. 'I mean, really hurt them—not just a bump or a bruise. I'm talking about snapping a limb or bashing in a head, or even'—she lowered her voice—'loss of life.'

Emily loved the run-up to Christmas, it was like the start of a poem: spicy cinnamon and glints of gold, green leaves and red robes, fairy lights and children singing. Even in the final scramble, in the week before everything shut down, when people frenziedly bought presents they couldn't afford and drank too much at office parties, she always tried to remain cheerful and calm. Now, standing at the entrance to an enchanted forest, on the third floor of a department store in London, dressed in a red robe with a hood, carrying a wicker basket, she tried to be helpful. 'I suppose you could hit them really hard with a cricket bat?'

'I think you misunderstood me,' said Miranda. 'I'm not suggesting you deliberately injure a child. I'm asking you to consider how a child could be injured by accident. In there.' She pointed into the dark interior of the forest, where exotic flowers had bloomed overnight, where the gnarled limbs of almost-human trees joined protectively over a meandering pathway that led to Santa's grotto, where gold and silver baubles were strung up among strands of twinkling white lights that threaded through the branches.

'Oh,' said Emily. 'I see ... Well, could they be electrocuted by the fairy lights? Injured by something falling from a tree?'

Miranda nodded. Emily was on the right track.

As is so often the way in briefing meetings, other members of the staff joined in now they knew what they were supposed to say. Unlike most staff meetings, however, everyone present was dressed as a character from a fairy tale.

Ray—a woodcutter—thought that shards of glass from broken Christmas tree baubles might get embedded in little fingers. He thought that trailing wires from plug sockets might trip tiny feet, or bits of scenery might poke any part of the body, but especially the eyes.

'Yes!' said Miranda. 'It's our job to protect them from all that.'

Ray adjusted his green felt Robin Hood hat so it sat at a jauntier angle, the pheasant's tail feather stuck in the side of it tickling the ends of his cornrows. Ray was a meaty young man who liked to work out in the gym four times a week. His big brown arms were sinewy and strong; he stood with his thick legs planted wide apart. He looked like a tree that had dressed up as a woodcutter. He shrugged and rolled his mahogany eyes, to show that he didn't consider it his job to protect anyone 'from all that.'

Miranda pretended to be indifferent to his indifference. 'Anyone else?'

A centaur called Selena—the lower half horse, the upper half human, despite the long face— thought the children themselves might be the cause of trouble. There was a rumble of dissent from the group, but Selena was adamant. 'Seriously, guys, it's nonsense to believe that children are inherently good. They fight and cheat and steal and tell tales.'

Emily wondered if Selena wasn't getting children mixed up with cowboys.

'We want the children who pass through the forest to be transformed by the experience—but only in a good way,' said Miranda. 'That's all I'm saying.'

'It would be great if it did transform them,' said Selena. 'Imagine that. Like, if Santa was real. You bring a few naughty kids and walk them through the forest, Santa has a chat with them, and they come out well-behaved.'

'Or politicians!' said Ray. 'Or bankers.'

'We'd be famous!' said Selena.

Miranda gave herself a little hug. 'You know what? When I was at art school, I might have wished for fame—or notoriety. But then I grew up. I've got friends who sell their work for millions. But I'd much rather spend my time on community projects, summer festivals, a few commercial installations like this one. Because for half an hour or so, as they go through it, the children believe the magic is real. If I could have one wish for all of us, to celebrate our hard work, it would be that—just for one night—we could believe it too.'

'I'd rather be rich,' said Ray.

'Me too. Sorry,' said Selena. 'What about you, Emily? What would you ask Father Christmas for?'

'No need to ask,' Emily said. 'He always brings me the same things: a chocolate orange, a pair of long socks and a puzzle.'

Miranda laughed. The group started to pick up their coats and bags to show they were ready to leave. It was so late already.

But Miranda had another strange question before she would let them go. 'Do any of you know any children?' She stared beseechingly around the group. She might have been asking, 'Do you know anyone from Bhutan?' as if children lived in an isolated kingdom a long, long way away from London, and it was impossible to meet them under normal circumstances.

'You don't need to worry about finding children to see Santa,' said Selena. 'The store will do that.'

'It's a tradition,' said Ray. 'People come with their kids year after year. You'll get plenty of bookings.'

They were pretending to reassure her, but really they were enjoying the smug feeling that follows the sudden realization that the person in charge is an idiot. It can make a pleasant end to a long day, unless that person is about to lead you into battle from out of the trenches.

Miranda tugged at the sleeves of her green jacket, irritated at their smugness. 'Yes. Yes, yes, yes. I know. We're fully booked as soon as it opens. But we need a child to test out the forest before then. It seems we've thought of everything, but we won't have. No matter how many times we walk through it, there's always something. You have to have a child to go through it. My niece was going to do it, but she's got chicken pox.'

Ray had a suggestion. He bent his knees and hunched down, resting his forearms on his big thighs. 'Couldn't we—'

Emily was horrified. Couldn't we what? Ray looked as if he was miming using the toilet.

'I know what you're going to say,' Miranda held up her hand to cut him off. 'With a background in set design for the theatre, she was obviously better at interpreting mime than Emily was. 'Asking a short person's no good.' She sighed with the wearied air of someone who had tried asking short people to test out her Christmas installations many times in the past, and always found them wanting. 'Children have a different way of seeing things. So, does anyone know any children?'

As it turned out, the children they knew might as well have been in Bhutan. Selena had a baby, but the baby was too young to test the layout and functionality of the magical forest. The other staff were childless. They had neighbours. But none of the neighbours' children were quite the right age for this project. They had nephews and nieces, but the nephews and nieces were in Cornwall or Dorset or Birmingham or Glasgow.

Emily could see another problem, even if they identified a suitable child to test out the project. 'Won't they all be in school? It's Friday tomorrow.'

Miranda sighed again—at the selfishness of children, the inflexibility of the British educational system, the stupidity of her staff... Emily wasn't sure

Helen Smith

exactly. The sigh was all-encompassing. 'I think we could write a letter to the school, don't you? An educational visit. Think what the child would learn.'

To be fair to Miranda, she was right. Helping to create the magical forest had been the best job Emily had ever had, like a form of extreme gardening. She had learned a lot. For the last five days, all day and late into the night, Emily had worked among craftspeople and technicians hammering, sawing, painting and stitching to create something magical and beautiful. And now it was finished, children would wander along the path that led to Santa, ushered by staff dressed as characters from fairy tales, accompanied by a responsible adult, choosing one piece of gold or silver fruit from the overhanging branches of the trees above the pathway and trading it for a gift from Santa.

Along the way, to keep them entertained, they would pass by oversized musical boxes and cabinets that could be operated when the child turned the handle. The cabinets were filled with all sorts of wonders: dancing automata, films glimpsed through peepholes, shadow puppets, talking birds. Tickets were expensive. The chance to wander through this place, almost alone, for free, would be a wonderful experience for a child of the right age. But where were they going to find that child at such short notice?

'Could we offer a kind of golden ticket?' said Ray. 'The kid who wins it gets to come in and explore the forest before it opens.'

'No,' said Miranda.

Then Emily had a clever idea. One thing you must never do at work is have a clever idea. If you do have one, you need to keep quiet until the urge to share it passes. Emily should have known better. She really should. 'There's a neighbour of mine, he lives at the end of the street. Harry. He's a retired Head Gardener and we're friendly because he gives me tips on my garden, though I don't know him well. Anyway, he said he doesn't see enough of his granddaughter, Sophie. I'm sure she lives in London. She started school last year so she must be about six years old. At that age, it wouldn't matter much if she missed the last day of term. And Harry would be so pleased if he could spend the day here with her.'

'Perfect! You talk to Harry, tell him to ask the parents' permission, find out the name of the school. Call me tonight, OK? We open on Saturday, so this has to happen tomorrow. I'll write an e-mail to the head teacher and tell her Sophie needs to have the afternoon off. It's a win for everyone. Sophie and Granddad get a tour of the forest; we show them how we transformed this place, and how this place can transform two ordinary people into two adventurers exploring an enchanted forest. We get a dress rehearsal. They get a magical experience, and they get to spend time together. What could go wrong?'

With all permissions duly granted, the next day Harry collected his granddaughter from school just after lunch and brought her to Oxford Street on the 137 bus. They sat at the top at the right-hand side, directly above the driver, and enjoyed a lovely view of London as they made their way through tree-lined streets to the magical place where the branches of the trees were hung with gold and silver baubles.

December in London is not nearly as miserable as January or February. In January and February, the rain is too wet, the air is too cold, and the days are too short. In December, there's a bite of cold in the air, but it's a puppy nipping playfully at your mittened hand, rather than the fully grown savaging of the later months. And when it's sunny in December, London's beauty sparkles. That day, as Harry and Sophie travelled on the bus through London together, it was sunny.

Sophie didn't talk much, so Harry talked. He pointed out places of interest: Battersea Park, with its Peace Pagoda, its boating lake and its fragrant rose garden; Chelsea Physic Garden, created by apothecaries in the seventeenth century to grow medicinal plants; Marble Arch with its nose-diving horse head statue; and Tyburn Covent with its enclosed order of nuns. He reminisced about what London was like in the old days, when he was a boy. The red buses didn't have a door on the back—you could jump on and jump off at any point along the route, although you weren't supposed to. He remembered running after a bus through the traffic with his two best friends, racing to catch up with a bus, jumping aboard and getting told off by the conductor. And, of course, you could smoke upstairs on the top deck. Everything he described sounded so wicked and wrong and old fashioned, as if people back then were trying to harm themselves deliberately. Could Sophie even understand what he was talking about?

But she listened solemnly and nodded. A couple of times she said, 'I'd like to do that!'

He wondered if she meant she'd like to run through moving cars to jump onto a bus, or jump off into the traffic. Or was it the smoking she liked the sound of? He wouldn't get many more opportunities to spend time with Sophie if she went back to her mother and told her that. Fortunately, the excitement of a stroll through the magical forest and meeting Santa should give her plenty of positive things to talk about when she got back home.

Emily was waiting for them when they arrived. So was Miranda. Emily was dressed in her red, hooded cape. Miranda was dressed in a green tunic, green pointed shoes, green tights and false ears. She was accompanied by a large poodle whose fur had been styled to make him look like a reindeer. He was wearing antlers and an embroidered saddle. Miranda was carrying an aerosol can of cinnamon-scented spray.

'Is that your poodle?' Emily asked her as they waited.

Miranda gave the air an excited squirt of cinnamon. 'Use your imagination! He's not a poodle. He's a reindeer.'

An elderly, creaky-looking man with rheumy blue eyes approached them, with a small, blond child of about six years old.

Miranda whispered, 'Showtime!'

Emily was to greet each child in a warm and friendly manner, ask the name and confirm the spelling with the adult accompanying them, then write the name on a sticky label and press it firmly to the child's coat, on the left-hand side near the shoulder. This would allow Father Christmas to greet the child by name, giving the illusion that he had been keeping up with their good deeds and misdemeanours. It would remind the responsible adult accompanying the child that they were not anonymous. The name would be checked off against a list of prebooked tickets. There was no readmission.

So this was the procedure Emily followed now. She greeted Harry and asked his granddaughter her name. Harry touched the little girl lightly on the shoulder, to get her attention—his hands were knobbly with rheumatism.

The little girl had been petting the reindeer poodle, but she stopped and gave her name. 'Sophie.'

Emily wrote the name on a label and stuck it to the child's coat. From a basket on the table next to her, Emily took a sealed letter addressed to Father Christmas, which was to be delivered by the child to the woodcutter. This letter allowed entry to the forest.

There would be several woodcutters dotted around the forest. Their job was to help the young child remove the dangling bauble once they had selected it from whichever branch of whichever tree they wanted—and, of course, ensure that only one was taken.

'It's difficult to see woodcutters as heroes, isn't it?' said Miranda, as they watched Sophie hand over her letter to Ray. 'With deforestation and everything.'

From deep within the forest, they heard the sound of Santa trying out the acoustics in his grotto. 'Ho ho ho!'

Miranda rolled her eyes. 'Sounds like a drunken uncle at a family gathering—not even a proper uncle, a former neighbour that everyone calls uncle out of respect, and now the respect has gone. I didn't want Santa, to be honest. A whiskery old man squatting in the middle of my forest asking impertinent questions of children about their behaviour. What's that all about? I'd much rather have had a Fairy Godmother. But the store owners insisted. Do you think little Sophie will choose a gold bauble or a silver bauble?'

'Gold? I don't know.'

'There's a perceived difference in value, but the gifts all cost about the same, of course. I'm doing a study to see how the choices break down on gender lines. Do you know the most useful thing I learned when I was at art college?'

Emily tried to remember the most useful thing Miranda had taught her over the past few days. 'Welding?'

'How to apply for funding. I should get a little extra money from a university for this study. You want to come to the security booth? You can meet my godmother.'

Miranda had a fairy godmother?

'She'll be watching the CCTV to make sure my study's set up properly.'

Miranda had a fairy godmother who kept watch on people via CCTV? Of course Emily wanted to meet her. She followed Miranda to the security booth.

On the way, Miranda tried to justify the use of cameras. 'With the low lighting in the forest, you'd be surprised how many people are tempted to steal—both staff and members of the public. And then there are the various hazards. You'll have children pulling down fairy lights, poking themselves in the eye with sharp objects, walking into walls in the poorly lit grotto, rolling out of control on their wheely shoes. And then there are the pranks. Every year, in a project like this, someone plays some sort of prank. It's not always malicious, but seasonal work attracts disgruntled staff. Students. They think they're better than the job on offer. You know the sort of thing. A partridge in a pear tree replaced by a penguin.'

Emily couldn't help it. She giggled.

'And, of course, we have to make sure no child gets separated from its parent. Have you ever lost a child, Emily?'

She hadn't.

'Even if it only happens for five minutes, it's absolutely the worst thing. For those five minutes, you can't promise yourself you'll ever see the child again.'

Miranda had that carelessness that often came with creativity. Emily took a moment to wonder how many children she might have lost over the years. Emily had never experienced anything like it herself, but she had seen it happen: the absolute still of the parent, like someone drowning, in the moment when the body shuts down, right before they sink beneath the waves. A few times she had lost sight of her dog, Jessie, in the park, and that had been bad enough. But when she called her, Jessie had always come bounding towards her with her big cheerful golden retriever smile.

'Fortunately, in all the years I've been doing these things, I've only ever witnessed a happy outcome. The moment when the little lost hand of the child touches their parent's and everything's

OK... It's almost worth losing one in the first place, just to see that happen. Almost. But we're so well set up in here, with the cameras and the fairy-tale characters chaperoning them through the forest. They're not out of sight even for a moment. It's not going to happen.'

When they reached the security booth, Emily was delighted to see that Miranda's 'fairy godmother' was her old friend Dr. Muriel, a middle-aged professor who lived across the road from her in Brixton.

Dr. Muriel was delighted to see Emily, too. 'I'm helping Miranda with her bauble project. She planned the forest, she built it, she's running it, and she's even managed to wring some funding from the university for this study. If this project had been a pig, she'd have found a way to eat the whole thing,' she said proudly. 'What are you up to? Are you investigating something? Don't tell me there's going to be a murder!'

'There won't be a murder,' said Emily. 'It's Christmas.'

They settled down to watch Harry and Sophie explore the forest, guided by Ray. Miranda was excited as she explained what she had created to Dr. Muriel. 'We've got simple things dressed up to look complicated. Duplicates. Mirrors. Shadows. Optical illusions.'

They watched Sophie visit Santa. He was sitting in a honeycomb-shaped, dimly lit grotto on a large, red velvet throne. Naturally he was wearing a red robe and whiskers. He had a computer in front of him on a gold table shaped like a sleigh. The back of the computer screen had been embedded in a glittery white snow globe.

'Ho ho ho! Hello, Sophie. What would you like for Christmas?'

She thought for a few moments, then said, 'Something so I can do gardening.'

'Aw,' said Emily in the security booth.

'Have you been good this year, Sophie?' Santa asked. 'I'd better just check my records.' He typed on the keyboard in front of him and peered at the screen. 'Yes. Very good. Don't forget to choose one of the baubles from the trees on your way out. Open it up; you'll need to show what's written inside to the elves. Perhaps Granddad can help with the reading?'

'Are they real elves?' Sophie asked.

'Well,' Santa said cautiously, 'I can't say for certain. They look real enough to me. Of course, looks can be deceiving.'

'Do they do elf things?'

'Yes. Well, they hand over presents to children out the back there.'

Sophie nodded, satisfied. 'They must be real elves.'

For a moment, Emily lost sight of Sophie. But then there she was, standing next to Santa. Harry was standing behind them.

'Shall we take a photo, then?' Santa prompted.

Ray picked up a Bakelite camera as big as an encyclopedia, with a grapefruit-sized silver disc surrounding the flashbulb on top. The three of them blinked as he took the picture. Ray stepped back, wincing.

'That's going to get annoying,' said Dr. Muriel.

'I'll see if he can't adjust the settings on that piece of kit—modern technology in old-fashioned housing, it's easy enough to do. This is why we need a dress rehearsal before the crowds come in.' But Miranda seemed pleased with the way it was going.

'You see all that business with the computer screen? He wasn't really checking whether or not she'd been good.'

'I should think not,' huffed Dr. Muriel.

'He makes a note of the gift the child says they'd like and e-mails it to the elves waiting at the back, so they can get it prepared. We've got the timing right, I think, though it's a bit tight.'

They watched as Harry and Sophie made their way out of the forest. Along the way, almost at the very last tree, Sophie stopped and pointed to a gold bauble. Ray used his plastic axe to help her snare it from the branch.

'Aha!' said Dr. Muriel. 'Gold. Very good.'

'Is it significant, do you think?' Miranda asked her.

'I don't know. Is it?'

Harry opened the bauble and read the number written inside. 'Seventy-two,' he said, peering at it in the darkness with his glasses. 'What do you suppose you'll get, then, Sophie?'

She shrugged.

'So it doesn't matter what the number is?' Dr. Muriel asked Miranda.

'Exactly! It's misdirection. Harry and Sophie will make their way to the edge of the forest, and Sophie will trade in her bauble to collect a gift from the elves. And it will seem amazing to her—and to most of the adults, I guarantee you—that whatever bauble she chose has a number inside that matches so closely the gift she told Santa she wanted. It doesn't even matter if a child asks for a puppy and gets a toy one. The magic of it, the way someone seems to have listened, the way the child herself is in control of the outcome because of the choice she's made, it's enough to make them feel very happy. You know, if this study goes off OK, Aunt Muriel, I'd be happy to come along to the university to do a talk about it.'

But Miranda's self-congratulatory daydreaming was interrupted by a phone call.

'There's a problem,' she said. 'We need to go down there.'

'What is it?' said Emily. 'Is Harry all right?' Maybe the excitement had been too much for him.

'Come and see,' said Miranda. She looked alarmed—frightened, even, as she led the way to the elves' station at the back of the forest.

'I'd like to report a missing child,' said Harry when they got there.

'What do you mean?' said Emily. 'Which child?'

He indicated Sophie. 'This child.'

'She's standing right next to you!' said Miranda. 'She's not missing!'

'This isn't the child I came in with.' Harry adjusted his glasses. 'She looks like Sophie. But this isn't Sophie.'

A small crowd had gathered. Ray was there. Selena was there. Dr. Muriel, Emily and Miranda were there. There were gasps when they heard what Harry had to say.

'You're confused, Harry,' said Miranda. 'It happens to the best of us. I look at my own face in the mirror some days, I hardly recognise it.'

'What's your name, dear?' Dr. Muriel asked the child.

'Sophie.'

Sophie was wearing the sticky label Emily had written for her. She looked exactly the same, except that she was carrying a cardboard box with a picture of a plant pot with a gaudy red amaryllis flowering in it, and she had a utility belt around her waist kitted out with small-sized gardening tools, including a trowel and a fork—the elves had done their job well this afternoon. The amaryllis was a particularly good choice. Strong green shoots would start growing from the bulb almost as soon as Sophie took the pot out of the box and watered the soil. Emily knew because she used to get one from her grandmother every year when she was around the same age. Wait! Why was she suddenly thinking about her grandmother? Emily drew her red cloak around herself and shivered, spooked at the recollection of such an old memory.

Dr. Muriel continued with her gentle questioning. 'And is this your grandfather, Sophie?'

Sophie shook her head. 'No.'

There was a lot of murmuring from the crowd at that. 'No!' 'No?' 'She said no!'

Sophie seemed upset that anyone would doubt her. 'You can ask Santa, he knows me. I haven't got a granddad.'

'She's been substituted!' whispered Selena. 'Aliens or... or some mischievous spirit dematerialized the child while she was in the forest, and put back one that was the same size, but slightly different.'

'I think there's probably an easier explanation,' said Dr. Muriel. 'What do you think, Emily? You're good with puzzles.'

'They're twins,' suggested Ray.

'Both called Sophie?' said Dr. Muriel.

Ray shrugged. 'It's a popular name.'

Dr. Muriel didn't know whether to be exasperated or entertained. 'Now, Ray, it really would be a failure of imagination for parents of twins to name both of them Sophie.'

'I'm sure this is the little girl Harry came in with,' said Emily. 'She looks exactly the same. That's my handwriting on the label on her coat.'

Miranda said, 'Sophie, do you remember seeing a reindeer when you came in?'

Sophie placed her amaryllis-in-a-pot on the floor next to her, carefully. She folded her arms and shook her head.

'Oh, this is awful,' wailed Miranda. 'If only my niece didn't have to be in her school play today. This disaster could have been avoided. It'll be all over the papers if we've lost a child here.'

Emily was suddenly suspicious. Miranda couldn't have staged this for the notoriety she said she'd grown out of wanting, could she? 'I thought you said your niece had chicken pox?'

'Something like that. School play, chicken pox... I can't remember exactly. I just know it's something that would be intensely irritating if I had to endure it.'

'Is this a stunt?' said Emily. 'A prank—like substituting the penguin for the partridge in the pear tree?'

'No!' Miranda seemed to be in earnest. 'Something like this, it's more than a prank with a penguin, which, I'll admit to you now, I carried out. I thought it might be a bonding experience for the staff. This isn't a prank! With a child reported missing, someone will want to call the police, they'll want to take Sophie away—and Christmas will be ruined. Has anyone called them yet? I do hope not. Ray, can you ask security not to call the police, please.'

'They have to call the police within fifteen minutes if a child's reported missing,' said Ray. 'It's protocol.'

'But she's here! She's right here!' Miranda grabbed hold of the child. 'Sophie, you must remember the reindeer.'

Sophie said, 'I only remember the dog.'

'Yes! Yes! You see? It is the same child you came in with, Harry. She remembers the poodle. This is your granddaughter.'

'No, she isn't.'

'I'm going to call the school, Harry. I'll get Sophie's head teacher on the phone. Maybe she can talk some sense into you.'

As Miranda stepped away from the group to call Sophie's head teacher, Emily said, 'Sophie looks the same to me. Harry, you're the one who looks different.'

'Ooh!' Selena liked that idea.

Miranda, midway through calling Sophie's school, stopped dialling and waved the phone to get Emily's attention. 'No! Seriously. One missing person is enough. Don't start with that.'

'Did you collect the picture you had taken with Santa?' Emily asked Sophie.

Sophie shook her head. She hadn't.

Emily smiled at her. 'I think we should take a look at it.'

Selena just about whinnied with excitement. 'You think Santa's responsible! That's brilliant. It's got to be him. He did it.'

Dr. Muriel didn't share Selena's enthusiasm. 'An out-of-work actor in a red robe and whiskers? How?'

Selena looked down, pawing at the ground with her shiny hoof, as if she expected to uncover a clue etched into the vinyl on the floor. Then she tossed her head back. 'Magic camera?'

'Ah,' said Dr. Muriel politely. 'Interesting theory.'

'Not as crazy as it sounds,' said Ray. 'He coulda made the switch when everyone was blinded by the flash.' He swung his axe. 'You want me to make a citizen's arrest? Hold him 'til the police come?'

'I don't think that will be necessary,' said Dr. Muriel, recoiling slightly as Ray brandished the plastic weapon. 'If he's guilty of something and he tries to escape, he won't get very far in that getup. The police will easily recognize him.'

'How long have we got?' asked Emily. 'Until the police are called?'

Ray looked at his watch. 'About ten minutes.'

'Would you mind getting the photo?' Emily asked him. 'The printer's by the elves' station.'

'Do you need the ten pounds?' Harry opened his wallet. 'I think you have to pay for it.'

'It's OK, Harry,' said Emily.

'If you get any trouble from the elves, you can tell them you're commandeering the photo,' Dr. Muriel said to Ray. 'For evidence.'

Ray slapped the flat of the plastic axe into the palm of his hand, to show that he was ready to tackle anything, even recalcitrant elves. Off he went to get the photo.

The photo was eight inches by six inches, full colour, in a clear plastic wallet. Ray passed it to Selena. Selena held it up next to Sophie. Same girl. Same face. Selena and Ray seemed disappointed. Selena passed the photo to Emily. She examined it. Santa was sitting in a chair, Sophie at his side, Harry behind them. Sophie looked exactly the same.

'That's the child Harry came in with,' said Emily.

But still, something didn't look right to her. Harry was different somehow. 'I know what it is! You're not wearing your glasses in the photo, Harry. I don't think you had them on when you came in, either. But you're wearing them now.'

Harry removed his glasses. He looked at Sophie. 'You look blurrier,' he said to her. 'More like my granddaughter.'

'There we are,' said Dr. Muriel. 'No harm done. Miranda! We've solved the mystery. This is Sophie—Harry just didn't recognise her because he came out of the forest with his glasses on.'

But Miranda walked towards her slowly, carefully, as if the ground was giving way beneath her feet. Her mouth was open. Her eyes were blank. If this was her happy face, Emily didn't ever want to be around when she heard bad news.

'Whatever's the matter with you?' Dr. Muriel asked her. 'You look as though you've seen a ghost.'

Miranda took a deep, calming breath and exhaled slowly. 'I talked to the head teacher. She just checked the classroom, and... Sophie's there.'

'So this isn't Sophie?'

'Unless she can be in two places at once,' said Ray.

'Whoa!' said Selena. 'Teleportation?'

Sophie smiled, innocently enough. But maybe the smile was a little... otherworldly.

'What is your name, dear?' asked Dr. Muriel.

'Sophie.'

Dr. Muriel turned to Emily. 'What do you think? Twins, aliens, ghosts, magic, teleportation?'

'Miranda said that a lot of the illusions inside the forest are simple things dressed up to look more complex. I think something like that has happened here.'

'You better come up with something quick,' said Ray. 'The police'll be here in'—he checked his watch—'about eight minutes.'

'OK. Let's start from the beginning. Harry told me he doesn't see his granddaughter very often. Her name's Sophie. She goes to a school not far from where we live. Harry got permission to take her out of school to bring her here to test the magical forest. He brought her here on the bus. I saw them both when they arrived. You guided them through the forest, Ray. They stopped and saw Santa, had their photo taken. When they came out of the forest to collect Sophie's gift, Harry thought his granddaughter looked different.'

'As though she'd been transformed,' said Miranda.

'What if we're all affected?' Selena made a nervous, whickering sound. 'I'm serious. Who's next?'

Emily shook her head. 'Sophie looked exactly the same to me when she came out of the forest as when she went into it. It was only when he put his glasses on that Harry realized she wasn't his granddaughter. Same build, same hair colour, same name. Close, but not quite right.'

'Ah,' said Dr. Muriel. 'How many girls in your class are called Sophie?'

Sophie held up her right hand. She unfurled one finger, two, three.

Emily nodded. 'He had gone to the school and told them he had permission to collect a child called Sophie, and they produced a little girl called Sophie—someone's granddaughter. Just not yours, Harry.'

Miranda rang Sophie's head teacher, putting her on speakerphone for the benefit of the group.

She sounded frantic. 'I can't talk now, Miranda. A child's gone missing at the school.'

'About four foot tall, six years old, blonde,' Dr. Muriel called out to her. 'Name of Sophie? I think we can help with that.'

'I'll bring her back on the bus now,' said Harry. 'If her mother agrees.'

'Can you plant my flower with me?' Sophie asked him.

'If your mother agrees.'

'You know, you got your Christmas wish,' Emily said to Miranda, when the logistics for returning Sophie to the school had been agreed with the head teacher. 'For a while, people really did think the magic in the forest might be real. Or Selena and Ray did, anyway.'

'I didn't!' protested Ray.

'I did,' said Selena. 'I really did.'

'And you got your puzzle,' said Miranda to Emily.

Emily grinned at her. 'As always.'

'But I still haven't got a granddad,' said Sophie. For the first time that day, she looked as though she might cry.

'Well, I can't say for certain,' said Emily, 'but Harry looks like a granddad to me. He acts like a granddad, travelling on the bus with you and offering to help you plant your amaryllis. So...'

'Yes,' said Sophie, cheering up. She put her hand in Harry's. 'He must be real.'

'Did you notice how Selina seemed to get a bit more centaur-like, the more time she spent in the forest?' Emily asked Dr. Muriel.

'There was a good bit of whinnying,' admitted Dr. Muriel. 'And pawing the ground. Wasn't she doing that at the beginning?'

'No! Ray became more heroic. Harry got to spend time with Sophie. Sophie got her Grandad. Miranda got her wish. I got my puzzle. It almost makes me believe in magic.'

'Ha!' said Dr. Muriel. 'Almost.'

From out of the corner of her eye, Emily saw a small reindeer emerge from the forest and run across the room.

By the same author:

THE EMILY CASTLES MYSTERIES
Invitation to Die is a quintessentially English
murder mystery featuring an astutely drawn mix of
larger-than-life characters... The book is very funny
indeed... There seems to be a winning line on every
page.
The bookbag.co.uk

An intelligent, likeable contemporary heroine and a
clever plotline... Like a modern day Agatha Christie.
Just a Normal Girl in London

Quirky, whimsical, smart, and engaging... I flat-out
loved it. A must-read for romance readers.
*Connie Brockway, bestselling romance author and
two-time RITA award-winner*

I love Helen Smith's writing. Her brand of mystery,
shot through with clever observational humour and
the sharpest of wit, is something that's been missing
from the genre for far too long.
*Alex Marwood, Edgar award-winning author of
The Wicked Girls*

Entertaining, gripping and fast paced with laugh-out loud moments.
Bookfabulous

This book is full of great lines, I was giggling through the book.
Wall-to-Wall Books

Invitation to Die is a fast, funny, easy read with many enjoyable comic moments.
Mystery People

All crime fiction readers will find this a quick and fun read. Fans of MC Beaton's Agatha Raisin or Simon Brett's Mrs Pargeter series will enjoy the humour and slightly surreal quality of this novel.
Crime Fiction Lover

Delightful stuff.
Shots Magazine

By the same author:

ALISON WONDERLAND
Only occasionally does a piece of fiction leap out
and demand immediate cult status. Alison
Wonderland is one.
The Times

Smith is gin-and-tonic funny.
Booklist

BEING LIGHT
Smith has a keen eye for material details, but her
prose is lucid and uncluttered by heavy description.
Imagine a satire on Cool Britannia made by the
Coen Brothers.
Times Literary Supplement

This is a novel in which the ordinary and the
unusual are constantly juxtaposed in various
idiosyncratic characters... Its airy quirkiness is a
delight.
The Times

THE MIRACLE INSPECTOR
The Miracle Inspector is one of the few novels that everyone should read, it's a powerful novel that's masterfully written and subtly complex.
SciFi and Fantasy Books

Helen Smith crafts a story like she's the British lovechild of Kurt Vonnegut and Philip K. Dick.
Journal of Always Reviews

About the author:

 Helen Smith is a novelist and playwright who lives in London. She is the author of *Alison Wonderland*, *Being Light* and *The Miracle Inspector* as well as the *Emily Castles Mysteries*.

Made in the USA
Lexington, KY
27 August 2016